RAY OF NEW

(Ray Series #6)

E. L. TODD

Fallen Publishing

Ray of New

Chapter One

Ryker

The rooftop apartment in Manhattan was exactly as I remembered it. The skyline showed the towering buildings, the burning lights that could be seen from miles away. My old gym was right around the corner, and my favorite Chinese restaurant was just a block away. My furniture had been untouched for a year, smelling stale with inactivity.

But it was still home.

Leaving Seattle was the best choice for me, and I didn't have any regrets. My brother would go a great job taking over COLLECT, and my mom wouldn't be lonely with him around. Manhattan was my home before my dad got cancer. It's where I should be.

My phone rang in my pocket, so I pulled it out and spotted Liam's name on the screen. I already knew what he would say before I even spoke to him. I took the call. "Hey, man. What's up?"

"Is your ass back in town yet?"

I walked to the window with a grin on my face. I stared at the car lights as they sat in traffic on the busy street. "Yep. Got in a few hours ago."

"Perfect. Let's hit up Roger's. I haven't seen your ugly face in a year."

"It's just as ugly as it was before," I said with a chuckle.

"Nah. It's probably worse." He laughed before he hung up.

I was just about to return my phone to my pocket when it rang again. Rae's name popped up on the screen.

My heart stopped when I saw it, remembering the sound of her voice. We always used to send inappropriate texts back and forth, her ass and tits usually the subject. I knew exactly why she was calling, and I didn't want to deal with it. I'd left without a backward glance. I didn't even tell her I was leaving. I just handed over the company and took off.

I hit ignore and sent her to my voice mail.

It was a dick move. But I didn't want to discuss the elephant in the room. It was obvious why I left, clear as a blue sky. She was happy with Zeke, and I was happy for her—somewhat.

***

"Wow. You really do look like shit." Liam stood and extended his arms wide apart.

I stopped in front of him, keeping five feet between us. "We never did the hug thing, so do we need to start now?"

"Oh, come on. You know I missed you."

"I didn't miss you."

He rolled his eyes. "Shut the hell up. Yes, you did." He gave me a bear hug.

I chuckled and returned the embrace, patting him on the back. "Okay…I may have a little."

We sat in the booth, and Liam pushed the beer he ordered toward. "Dark—the way you like it."

I lifted my mug and tapped it against his. "You know me too well." I took a drink and let the beer slide down my throat and right into my gut. Alcohol was the only companion I'd had lately. I was drinking too much of it recently, and as a result, I had to work out twice as hard to keep my physique in check.

"I'm gonna say something, and it's gonna sound kinda douchey."

I set my frosty glass on the coaster and leaned back against the seat in the booth. I was used to the weird things Liam said, but I didn't realize how much I missed them until now. "I can handle it." I beckoned him with my hand. "Let's hear it."

"I'm sorry things didn't work out in Seattle…but I'm really glad they didn't. This city isn't the same without you."

"Yeah?" The corner of my mouth rose in a smile.

"Yeah," Liam said. "I haven't found a good wingman since you left. The guys are great, but they aren't smooth as you are."

"I'm sure you did just fine, Liam."

"Obviously." He took a drink before he returned it to the table. "Just not as fun. Remember that time we both got blow jobs on the Ferris wheel in Coney Island?"

I'd forgotten about that until now. "Oh, yeah…that was a great night."

"It really was," he said with a dreamy look on his face. "That chick had the biggest mouth. She talked a lot, but when it came to sucking—" His phone rang in his pocket, so he dug it out.

"You don't need to finish that sentence," I said with a laugh.

He glanced at the screen and rolled his eyes.

"You got a stalker, man?"

"Kinda. But not in a good way." He answered the call and pressed his phone to his ear. "Dude, what's up?"

A woman's voice came over the speaker. "Don't dude me. I've been living in the city for three days, and I still haven't seen you."

He rolled his eyes again even though she couldn't see him. "Take a chill pill, alright? I'm busy."

"And you think I'm not busy?" she countered. "And if you roll your eyes one more time, I'm gonna slap you."

I immediately glanced around and searched for a sassy woman with a phone to her ear.

Liam raised an eyebrow and tensed, looking out the window like she was lurking nearby. "Where are you...?"

"I'm not watching you, idiot. I just know you that well."

Liam sighed in relief and leaned against the cushion of the booth. "You creeped me out there."

"Come on, I want to see you. Can we get a beer or something?"

"Can't you get some friends or something?"

I had no idea who he was talking to. I couldn't tell if it was an old girlfriend or what.

"Shut up, Liam," she said over the phone. "I want to see you. I miss you."

He rolled his eyes.

"I saw that!"

"Geez, you're a freak. Fine, I'm at Roger's on Fifth. I'm with a friend."

"Okay." Her voice perked up. "I can't wait to see you!" She hung up.

He slid his phone away from him on the table. "Talk about a nightmare..."

"Who was that?" If it was a crazy girlfriend, he should be a little more freaked out.

"My sister," he explained. "She just moved to the city last week, and she's wanted to hang out."

"Oh." I knew he had a few sisters, but I never met her and he never mentioned her. "That's cool. Where did she move from?"

"Cambridge. She just graduated, and she got a gig at Nicol Software."

"I heard that's a great company."

"I heard that too. She's the new head of marketing." He shook his head. "Can you believe that?"

"And she just graduated college?" You can't just secure a high position right out of school without any real-life experience. At least, I'd never heard of that. Companies wanted someone who'd dealt with real-life problems.

"Yep."

"Is she a genius or something?"

"Something like that," Liam answered. "She graduated from MIT."

"Damn."

"Yeah." He finished his beer then waved down the bartender for another.

I pictured her with thick glasses, strange clothing, and an unusual demeanor. In my experience, really smart people were always awkward. They didn't pick up on social cues and saw the world in very different colors. "How are you guys related?"

"Ouch," he said. "I'm smart too."

"Not MIT smart."

He shrugged. "I'm not sure where she gets it from…" His eyes darted out the window and followed someone as they walked inside. "She's here. Man, she gets around fast."

I didn't turn around because that would be rude. "She probably built a jet pack or something."

Liam chuckled as he slid out of the booth. "No kidding." He rose to his feet and waved so she could see him. "Over here, dumbass."

"Liam!" His sister walked to the table, her heels clanking against the hardwood floor. When she emerged past my chair, I saw the skintight blue dress she wore. It was snug on her petite waist and slender thighs, and it hugged the obvious curves of her chest. She had deep brown hair that had a tint of red to it.

She was not at all what I pictured.

"I missed you so much." She hugged him to her chest with her arms around his neck, showing more enthusiasm for a sibling than anyone else in the history of time. "I haven't seen you in forever."

He patted her on the back. "That's not true. We saw each other—"

"Last Christmas. That was almost two years ago."

"Okay…maybe it has been a while." He pulled away and placed his hands in his pockets. "So, you like the city?"

"I love it," she said. "I have a few friends who live here, so they've been showing me around."

"Cool," he answered.

"Obviously, I would have preferred it if my brother showed me around, but you've been too busy." She poked him in the chest playfully.

"Guilty," he said with a shrug. "I'll get you something from the bar. Cabernet?"

"Yes, please." She flicked her hair behind her shoulder, the soft curls forming a curtain of silk down her back.

I still hadn't looked at her face, but I knew she wasn't wearing glasses.

"By the way, this is my friend, Ryker." Liam nodded to me in the booth. "Ryker, this is my sister, Austen. I'll be right back." He walked to the bar and left us alone together.

She turned to me and made an obvious reaction, just as surprised by my appearance as I was by hers. She caught her footing instantly and extended her hand. "It's nice to meet you."

I shook her hand. "You too."

She sat in the booth across from me and scooted over so there was room for Liam.

Now that I had a good view of her face, I noticed how different she looked in comparison to Liam. She had fair skin with a light sprinkling of freckles. She had a small nose and bright blue eyes that reminded me of a coral sea. Her hair was thick and shiny. A gold necklace hung around her neck, making me notice the hollow in her throat. I suddenly pictured myself kissing the area, tasting it with my curious tongue. My body immediately hummed to life just from looking at her, finding her sexy at first glance. Everything about her was perfect, from the natural beauty of her face to the way her short legs looked long because they were so fit and toned.

I usually had something to say, but now words failed me. I just stared at her, feeling my skin grow warm with searing heat. I saw beautiful women on a daily basis, but none of them made me lose my train of thought. She completely wiped my brain like it was a blank canvas. I could have made small talk and asked her where her apartment was or what she liked most about the city, but I couldn't even do that. I felt my cock harden in my jeans and press against the inside of my zipper. I couldn't even adjust myself because that would be too obvious with her sitting right across from me. I swallowed the lump in my throat so I could speak, but words still didn't emerge.

Austen was talkative with her brother a moment ago, but now she was just as quiet. She watched me with tension in her shoulders, her blue eyes glued to my face. For being two strangers, we made more eye contact than most people would feel comfortable with.

Luckily, Liam returned. "I almost ordered the whole bottle because I know you drink a lot. But then I remembered I'm broke. So here ya go."

She took the glass with a smile. "Thanks, Liam. I knew you missed me."

"I never said I missed you," Liam argued.

"But yet, you went up there and got me a glass of wine." She sipped her drink, pressing her soft lips together.

"Because I'm a nice guy," Liam said.

"But we both know you aren't a nice guy to everyone," Austen said. "So just admit you like me."

"Why would I dodge your calls if I liked you?" Liam rested his elbows on the table as he stared at her. "Answer that one."
She set her glass down as she savored the taste of the wine on her tongue.

I pictured myself tasting that wine all over her body.

She eventually answered. "You were too excited."

Liam shook his head. "No. It's because you're annoying."

"Yeah, okay," she said sarcastically. "Who's the one who would call me every Sunday while I was in school?"

Liam immediately wore a guilty face, his cheeks turning red. "I was just checking on you—"

"Whatever you say." She tried to suppress a smile, but it crept into her features. Her blue eyes were bright and playful, and there was an innate energy about her that made her magnetic. "I'm going bowling tomorrow night. You wanna come?"

"Who else is going?" Liam asked.

"Some friends of mine." She turned to me, her expression immediately changing once her eyes settled on my features. It wasn't clear if she was attracted to me or just intimidated. "You're welcome to come too."

"Wait," Liam said. "Are any of these friends hot?"

"I think so," she deadpanned. "But all my friends are cute."

"But are these nerdy friends?" Liam asked with a disgusted look.

"What's wrong with being a nerd?" she asked. "I'm a nerd, and I'm proud of it. I'm interested in the way things work. I want to know more information about subjects I don't understand. A quizzical mind is never a bad thing."

I smiled at her response, liking the way she defended herself and her friends.

"You know that saying?" Liam asked. "Curiosity killed the cat?"

"Well, I'm not a cat," Austen said. "So I'm in the clear."

"Ryker is kinda new to the city," Liam explained. "He lived in Seattle for a while for work until he came back."

"Oh, cool," Austen said. "Then you should come. We call our team the Bowling Stones."

I chuckled because I immediately got it. "Clever."

"Huh?" Liam asked. "The Bowling what?"

"Like the Rolling Stones," Austen explained. "But the Bowling Stones..."

Liam still wore the same confused expression.

"Never mind." Austen drank from her glass. "We have a bet going. Whoever loses has to go to a strip club and stick a hundred one-dollar bills into some G-strings while the winners watch."

"That doesn't sound like much of a punishment to me." I'd been to quite a few strip clubs in my day.

"Me either," Austen said. "But a hundred bucks is a lot of cash. So that sucks."

"I'm in," Liam said. "Your friends are single, right?"

"Yeah, but you know the rule." Austen held up a finger. "We don't date each other's friends. Remember?"

Liam made a sour face. "Who said anything about dating? If they're down for some good sex, then what's the big deal?"

Austen made a disgusted face and covered it up with her wine. "Don't chase away my friends, alright? Otherwise, I'll have to kick your ass."

"Ha," Liam said sarcastically. "Like you could."

She gave him a mean face, her eyes threatening and her jaw clenched.

She looked even sexier when she was pissed.

The look successfully intimidated Liam. "Alright, alright. I'll behave myself."

Chapter Two

I hung around my apartment and played video games and watched TV. I had no intention of getting a job when I had enough in my real estate investments to get me by. My father gave my brother and me a great deal of money when we were younger. My brother pissed his away, and I put my cash to good use.

So I didn't feel bad about it.

Rae left me a message the other night, but I still hadn't listened to it. I did my best not to think about her because anytime I did, I felt like shit. I had the perfect woman wrapped around my finger until I blew it by being the biggest asshole in the world. She told me she loved me, and I left her.

I got exactly what I deserved.

I wasn't jealous of Zeke. I wasn't angry at Rae. The only person I despised was myself.

It was all my fault.

My phone rang on the coffee table, but I didn't look at it right away. I expected to see Rae's name on the screen, the one person I didn't want to talk to but also desperately wanted to talk to.

I dragged my hands down my face then looked at the screen. It was a number I didn't recognize, and the area code wasn't from New York but it wasn't Washington either. So I answered. "Hey, it's Ryker."

"Hey, Ryker." A beautiful voice came over the phone, hypnotic and sexy. "It's Austen."

My heart immediately picked up its pace, and I felt my cock twitch in my sweatpants. I hadn't thought about her since I saw her in the bar the other night, but now that she was on my mind, I was hard. "What's up?" I kept my cool and leaned back against the couch.

"I got your number from Liam. Hope that's okay."

"Of course. I love it when beautiful women stalk me."

She chuckled. "Hope that doesn't happen too often."

"Not as much as I would like it to." I smiled and hit the mute button on the TV remote. "What can I do for you, Austen?" Was she calling about our bowling plans?

"I wanted to see if you were free tonight. I'd like to take you out."

My heart froze in my chest as my stomach tightened. Her confidence was insanely sexy. Not too many women would have the balls to call up a guy and ask him out like this. I preferred strong women who didn't care what anyone thought of them. I hadn't met too many like that. Austen seemed to fit in that category. "I'm flattered."

"And I'd be flattered if you said yes. We can go to a bar and watch the game."

I grinned. "That sounds like a pretty nice date, actually."

"I know. We can share a plate of garlic fries. So romantic."

I chuckled, feeling my chest loosen at her playful banter. As much as I wanted to say yes, Liam popped into my head. He was one of my closest friends and dating his sister would really piss him off. The last time I did that, I lost a friend altogether. I wasn't looking for a relationship anyway, so it wasn't worth going down this road. "I would love to say yes, but I can't."

"Damn. I knew you had a girlfriend..."

"Actually, I don't. But...I don't think it would be a good idea. Liam is my friend, and I have to honor the code."

"Fuck the code."

My eyes widened as the smile stretched my lips.

"Just come down and have a beer. Don't be a drama queen about it."

I laughed. "A drama queen?"

"Yeah. Liam doesn't need to know about it."

I wasn't really the kind of guy to sneak around. My life was an open book, so I had nothing to hide. When Rae and I kept our relationship a secret from Rex, I wasn't too thrilled about it.

"I'm not taking no for an answer. I'll meet you at the Frog's Tooth in an hour."

"Austen—"

"You better show up. Otherwise, I'm gonna eat all those garlic fries solo." Click.

I listened to the line go dead with the same smile on my lips. I didn't call her back because I had every intention of going.

I wasn't the kind of guy to stand up a lady.

***

After Rae went back to Zeke, I slept around for a while. I picked up women all over Seattle and brought them back to my place. Some of them were cool. Some were just pretty. But none of them meant anything to me.

I couldn't even remember their names.

I couldn't add Austen to the pile because that would be a dick move. But I was back in Manhattan, and I needed to get on with my life. I needed to have new relationships and new experiences so Rae would leave my thoughts forever. I didn't want to have to force myself not to think about her.

I wanted it to be natural.

I entered the bar a few blocks from my apartment and found Austen sitting at the counter on one of the stools. She wore a purple dress with matching heels on her feet. Her hair was straight today, and it was pulled over one shoulder. Even from behind, I could discern her luscious curves. She had a petite, hourglass frame. If I wrapped my hands around her waist, I suspected my fingers would meet. Her skin was fair like she didn't spend much time in the sun, but I liked its flawless appearance. She reminded me of a Barbie doll—supersexy.

I moved onto the stool beside her. "Hope all the fries aren't gone."

"Sorry, I couldn't wait. But I ordered another basket."

I couldn't tell if she was kidding or not, but either way, it didn't matter. "I'll catch up."

She had a beer in front of her, a lighter brew than I liked. It was halfway empty with her lipstick stained on the glass. It was red and vibrant, and I suddenly imagined that color stained around the base of my cock. "Are you a Knicks fan?"

It took me a moment to understand her question because I was picturing her on her knees in my bedroom. "Forever and always."

"Me too. The thing I love most about basketball is the camaraderie. Sometimes they make these incredible plays that are spontaneous and they can't be planned. And they work so well because all the players are so in tune with each other. It's fascinating to see that type of connection."

I stared at the dark makeup around her eyes and the way the blue color of her irises stood out. "That's a good observation. But I think other sports have that same kind of camaraderie."

"Some," she said in agreement. "I don't see it as much as in baseball. Honestly, I hate the sport."

My jaw nearly dropped. "You hate baseball? That's a crime against America."

She was about to drink her beer but chose to laugh instead. "It just takes too long to set up the action, you know? With basketball, you gotta watch every second. Otherwise, you might miss something. But with baseball…you could take a thirty-minute nap and still not miss anything."

"You've obviously never been to a game."

"I have," she said. "Big snoozefest."

"Wow." I shook my head in disappointment. "Just when I thought you were the full package. I guess everyone has an Achilles' heel."

"Full package, huh?" She smiled as she looked at me, her eyelashes thick. "I just ate a full basket of fries before you got here. I'm rude, and I'm a pig."

"This isn't a date, so you weren't rude. And if you're a pig, you're the sexiest pig I've ever seen."

She chuckled as her eyes lit up like stadium lights. "That's the nicest and strangest compliment I've ever received. And this is a date because I asked you out and you came. Boom, it's a date."

Her playful confidence only made me fonder of her. "Alright, it's a date. But I'm buying."

"Nope. You're dealing with a feminist. You've been warned."

"You're dealing with a gentleman. So you've been warned."

"My card is already on file, so that's too bad." She stuck out her tongue like a child, and while the action was juvenile, she still looked cute.

I shook my head in disappointment. "I guess I'll have to get you back some other time."

"And I hope you do."

I held her gaze as my cock came to life. I loved her playfulness. I hardly knew her, but she already felt like someone I'd known for a long time. Like she was one of the guys, I was watching a game with her at the bar. It was hard to believe she was truly a stranger. "Liam told me you graduated from MIT."

She rolled her eyes dramatically. "What else did he tell you about me?"

"That's you're a nerd."

She shook her head and whispered under her breath. "I'm gonna kick his ass."

I chuckled. "I think nerds are cute." I immediately thought of Rae, a chemical analyst at my family's company. Her intelligence was one of the attributes that attracted me in the beginning—besides her smokin' body. I pushed her out of my mind, doing my best to forget her and move on.

"Yeah?" Austen asked. "That bodes well for me."

"You don't look a nerd though. More like a supermodel."

She laughed as if I'd made a joke. "You're way too sweet. But I like that."

"I'm serious." I turned on my stool and leaned close to her, feeling my heart thump in my chest. She smelled like summer roses that had been freshly picked from the bush. "That's the first thing that popped into my head when I saw you."

"You thought I was a supermodel?" she asked incredulously.

"I definitely didn't think you were a nerd." My face was just inches from hers, and I wanted to kiss her. I wanted to feel her tongue in my mouth as she panted for me. I wanted to feel her up in the bar then get her back to my place. My sheets needed to be drenched in her smell so I could pretend she was still there long after she was gone.

But when Liam popped into my head, I found the strength to pull away. I couldn't fool around with his sister, especially when she was just a rebound. That would piss off Liam, and I wouldn't blame him.

Disappointment filled her gaze when I pulled away, but she quickly covered it up by taking a drink of her beer. "What do you do for a living?"

"Liam didn't tell you?"

"No. I didn't ask."

"In Seattle, I ran my family's garbage and recycling company. My brother took it over, so I came back here. I went to school at NYU."

"Oh, cool. So New York is your home?"

Seattle felt like home for a short while. "For the most part. Now I live off my investments and relax."

"So you're retired?"

"You could say that."

"Wow. You must be smart with your money to pull that off before you're thirty."

"I'm thirty-one."

"Liam is thirty, so I just assumed." The waiter dropped off another basket of fries, and she didn't hesitate to grab one and pop it in her mouth. She had plump lips and perfect teeth. I pictured myself sucking that bottom lip into my mouth and tasting the garlic on my tongue.

I needed to chill. "You're twenty-two?"

"Twenty-three."

She was a little young for me, but then again, I wasn't going to fuck her, so it didn't matter. "How are you liking Nicol?"

"I love it. Their software is so advanced that it boggles my mind. There's so many implications with it and so many ways to reach everyone around the world. They're a humanitarian company, creating jobs only in America and making large donations to people in need overseas. It's a remarkable company, and I'm honored to be a part of it."

"That's good to hear. If you love your job, you never have to work a day in your life."

"Exactly." She tossed another fry into her mouth. "You aren't going to make me eat all of this by myself, right?"

I grabbed a fry and dropped it into my mouth. "Of course not."

Her hand moved to my thigh, and she gave me a firm squeeze, her sharp nails digging into me slightly. "Looks like you are a gentleman, after all." She pulled her hand away and turned back to the TV, like she didn't just cause my dick to twitch.

I turned to the TV and tried to keep my pulse under control. I wasn't used to holding back and stopping myself from having what I wanted. If I wanted a woman, I just took her. But this woman was off-limits and untouchable. I wondered if that made me want her more, but I suspected that wasn't a factor.

The only reason why I wanted her was simple—because she was amazing.

Chapter Three

I walked into Liam's music shop and eyed the electric Fender guitars on display. One was creamy white with metallic strings. I'd played a few times, but I preferred the sound of an acoustic. It was much easier to hide my inadequacies when the music was being projected through a speaker.

"Yo." Liam left the counter and joined me in the showroom. "What brings you in?"

"Just thought I'd stop by and see if you wanted to get lunch."

"I'm not hungry, but I can always go for a beer."

"Beer. Lunch. Same thing."

Liam locked up the shop, and we walked to the deli just a few shops over.

"This is my favorite spot," Liam said. "They make their chips in the store, and they're the bomb. Like kettle chips, but better."

"I know," I said sarcastically. "We've been here before."

"Oh, yeah." He snapped his fingers. "Sorry, I'm not sure how I forgot that."

"Because you're an idiot."

We ordered our food and took a seat in one of the booths. Liam claimed he wasn't hungry, but he immediately shoved half the sandwich in his mouth like a T-Rex and swallowed it whole. He had dirty-blond hair that was far lighter than mine and an athletic build. He'd just shaved that morning, so his small beard was gone.

"How's the shop?"

"I'm getting by. That's how it's been for years."

"No ups or downs?"

"Christmas is always a good season, but other than that, it's pretty much the same. The thing with musical instruments is they're so expensive that people only buy what they need, like, once every few years. So sales are hard to come by. But if I do sell a drum set or a guitar, it's a big sale."

"Gotcha."

"But I'd rather barely get by doing what I love than make a lot of money doing something I hate. That's just me."

I didn't care for working for COLLECT. It was all phone calls, business meetings, and doing the payroll. It definitely wasn't exciting. The best part of my day happened when I went downstairs to the lab and spoke to Rae. "I know what you mean."

"So are you going to get a job or anything?"

I shook my head. "I doubt it. I might do electric stuff for COLLECT to help out my brother here and there, but other than that, no."

"See?" He shoved another piece of his sandwich into his mouth, taking a few minutes to chew it. "We're the same. We don't work hard—we work smart."

I nodded. "Yep."

"So, did you leave a woman behind?"

I'd mentioned Rae a few times to him, but I always said it wasn't serious. I never told him how I screwed everything up like the damn idiot I was. "No."

"What happened to that one chick you mentioned?"

I threw a chip into my mouth and felt it crunch between my teeth. "Damn, these are good. I haven't eaten chips in forever."

"I know, right? If I weren't looking for Ms. Right, I'd eat this shit every day."

"For Ms. Right, huh?" I waggled my eyebrows. "Looking to settle down?"

He shoved a handful of chips into his mouth and took forever to chew and swallow. "I've been thinking lately...I'm thirty. I'm kinda at the end of my fun phase. All the good chicks are getting scooped up. I've got, maybe, five years left before I just look like an old, single weirdo. So I need to find a good catch while there's still some good fish left."

I nodded in agreement. "I see your point."

"What about you? Are you thinking about getting married and junk?"

"And junk?" I asked with a laugh.

"Yeah. A wife. A picket fence. Little brats running around. You know the drill."

From the way he described commitment, it didn't seem like he was looking forward to it. "You don't make it sound that appealing."

"It's better than being alone, right? My married friends tell me they felt the same way I do. But once they found the right woman, there was nothing else they wanted more. So, I'm gonna put some faith in that and start looking for Ms. Right."

I was just relieved we changed the subject from Rae. But when I thought of forever, she was the only woman I pictured myself with. Unfortunately, I'd realized what I wanted too late. Six months came and went. I was stupid for waiting around that long.

"So?"

His question brought me back to reality. "So, what?"

"Marriage a possibility for you?"

"Are we gossip girls now?" I asked with a chuckle.

He shrugged and kept eating. "It's something I think about a lot. I think all guys think about it at some point in their lives. I'm guessing your answer is no?"

Relationships were too difficult for me. I wasn't even sure how I had anything great with Rae. I never really let my walls down for her when I should have. And like I feared, I ended up hurting her when I tried to avoid it. I wasn't fit to be a husband, not even a boyfriend. I was too fucked up in the head, too depressed, and too hopeless. "It's not for me."

"Not ever?" he asked incredulously. "You're gonna be a fifty-year-old guy picking up chicks at bars?"

I smiled and pointed at my face. "I'll always have the charm."

"Okay, what about when you're sixty?"

I shrugged. "I think I'll still have some talent then."

"Okay...seventy?"

That was my limit. "When I'm seventy, then I guess I'll go back to jerking off. But I'll probably have arthritis, so maybe it'll hurt too much."

He chuckled before he grabbed a few more chips. "See? That's when you'll need a wife."

"She'll probably have arthritis too."

"But she'll do it anyway—because that's what marriage is all about."

***

Liam and I walked to the bowling alley in jeans and t-shirts. Even though it was after eight, the humidity of the city was still unbearable. I usually stayed indoors during the hottest time of day just to beat the heat.

"I hope my sister has some sexy friends. If she doesn't, I'm gonna turn around and walk out."

"You will not."

"You bet your ass I will. If they're gross, I'm taking a hike."

"Gross or not gross, a blow job is still a blow job."

Liam shrugged in understanding. "Yeah, I guess you're right. I'll lower my standards for the evening."

"And what makes you think your sister has ugly friends? In case you haven't noticed, she's a beautiful girl." The words slipped out of my mouth before I could think twice. At least I didn't admit I wanted to nail her.

Liam didn't seem to care about the compliment I just gave. "I guess that's true. Girlfriends seem to be about the same level."

"So we should be good."

We walked inside and headed to the lanes. The sound of bowling balls speeding down the lanes and colliding with the pins filled my ears. I was immediately brought back to another time when I went bowling with Rae and her friends. She and I had just taken our relationship to a new level of exclusivity.

I forced the thoughts out of my head.

"They're over there." Liam walked with his hands in his pockets, checking out the girls since they were all looking at the screen and entering their names. "Ooh…they're all cute. What are the odds?"

The blonde was dressed in washed-out jeans with holes in the knees. She wore a t-shirt with a zebra on it with lots of gold bangles and necklaces. Her hair was in spirals, and she looked like a model for H&M. The other had olive skin with jet-black hair. She wore black leggings with a pink sleeved shirt that only covered one shoulder. They were both lookers—but they paled in comparison to Austen.

"Why the hell didn't my sister tell me about this before?"

"In her defense, she's been trying to get together with you since she moved here."

"Don't take her side, alright? I deal with that enough with my folks." He walked down the steps and raised his arms in the air. "The party has arrived, ladies." He walked right up to the girl in the pink and extended his hand. "Liam. I'm a musician."

She smiled and shook his hand. "Madeline. I'm a dancer."

"Ooh..." Liam rubbed his hands together. "Like...a topless dancer?" He couldn't keep the hope out of his voice. "The kind that knows how to work a pole?"

I didn't have a clue how Liam picked up ladies. His moves were abrasive and suffocating. Apparently, women found him charming.

"Ballet," she said with a distinct British accent.

"Ooh..." Liam cringed when he realized he'd shoved his foot in his mouth. "That's cool too...totally cool."

She chuckled then turned to me. "Madeline. And you are?"

"Ryker." I shook her hand and didn't ask if she was a stripper. It was pretty easy. "Nice to meet you."

The blonde came next, her bracelets making a quiet clicking sound she moved. "Jenn. Which one of you is Austen's brother?"

"That would be me." Liam raised a hand like a student in a classroom. "Growing up with a woman has really taught me about women…their needs and their feelings. You know, I'm pretty sensitive."

Somehow, I found the strength not to roll my eyes and walked over to Austen. Liam was busy making an idiot of himself to the girls, so I knew our conversation wouldn't be overheard. She was in jeans and a skintight t-shirt, the curves of her body obvious and beautiful. "Hey, Stone Cold."

She turned away from the screen and scrunched her eyebrows like she didn't have a clue what I was saying. "Excuse me?"

"You know, Steve Austin. The wrestler."

She released a loud laugh when she finally got my joke. "Stone Cold Steve Austin…I've been called by a lot of names but never that one."

"You seem pretty badass, so I think it fits."

"Badass, huh?" She typed her name into the line on the machine. Instead of putting her first name, she wrote Steven Austin.

I grinned from ear to ear. "I'm glad you're embracing it so well."

"Sometimes things just click." She typed in the names of the rest of the crew. "And what name should I put for you?"

"Ryker always works."

"How about…" She typed in Hawt.

I raised an eyebrow. "I don't get it."

"Sound it out."

I said the word out loud then realized it was a play on the word hot. "Oh…gotcha. That's awfully generous."

"Especially after I write this…" She typed in her brother's name. "Chicken Butt."

"Hmm…I never really thought he looked like a chicken."

"But he smells like one." She typed in a sixth name. Jared.

Another guy was joining us, and I immediately wondered if it was a date she'd brought along. A momentary flash of jealousy washed through me, but once I realized how misplaced it was, I shook it off. "Who's the sixth guy?"

"My bestie. He's in the bathroom." She hit the start button, and the lanes unlocked.

A good-looking guy who was as tall as I was came down the stairs in jeans and a t-shirt. It was obvious he worked out—daily. He had a nice smile, stubble along his jaw, and shoulders that rivaled mine.

Please be gay.

"Liam, right?" He shook his hand. "I'm Jared. Looks like we're up against a bunch of girls."

"I hope you're good at bowling because I'm not," Liam said. "But I don't mind going to a strip club, so I guess it's fine."

"It's a dude strip club," Jared explained.

Liam immediately cringed. "Oh…then we better win."

Jared came to me next and shook my hand. "Jared."

"Ryker." I quickly dropped his hand, feeling threatened by the guy when I didn't know him. He didn't seem gay, so that made me automatically dislike him. Austen referred to him as her best friend, but he was straight? What was that about? "Nice to meet you."

"You too. Any good at bowling?"

"I'm okay," I answered. "I'm sure I'm good enough to beat them."

He chuckled. "The girls are pretty good, actually. We'll have to step it up."

***

Austen was awesome.

For a petite woman, she had a great arm on her. When she didn't roll strikes, she got spares. She had the highest score of all of us, and the rest of the girls had great scores on top of that.

"We're getting our asses handed to us," Liam said. "But you know what? I don't care. Makes them so much hotter."

"Madeline is small, but she's pretty strong," Jared said. "She's a dancer, so her core is unbelievable." He eyed Madeline sitting at the other table, his eyes glued to her face.

I couldn't tell if he was into Austen or not, but it seemed like he had a thing for Madeline.

And I was relieved.

At the end of the game, we lost by fifty points.

It was embarrassing.

"Hell yeah." Austen did a dance in her bowling shoes, throwing her hands in the air and shaking her hips. The girls jumped in, dancing around and having a good time. "We kicked ass, ladies. Now it's time to head to the strip club."

Liam leaned toward me and whispered under his breath. "Do we seriously have to do that?"

"Yep," Jared said. "I've made Austen do it. But, between us, I think she liked it more than she should."

I smiled when I pictured Austen sticking one-dollar bills in women's G-strings. And, of course, I got hard too. "I've never been to a male strip club. I guess there's a first time for everything."

***

I turned my cash into one-dollar bills at the bar then returned to the table where everyone was sitting. I tossed my stack of bills onto the table as I sat down, a male stripper working the small stage right in front of us.

Madeline raised her arms in the air and released a scream. "Work it, baby."

"I wish I could dance like that," Austen said. "He works his hips better than I do."

I pictured her in only a thong dancing just for me. I sat on the couch in my living room with all the lights off while she gave me a private show. Naturally, I was a sexual person. But Austen pushed the boundaries of my sexuality. She ignited my imagination, making me fantasize things because I couldn't have the real thing.

"Alright, boys." Jennifer rubbed her forefinger and thumb together. "Work those bills."

Liam stared at the male dancer then dragged his hands down his face. "I don't want to touch him..."

"We made a bet," I reminded him. "We have to keep it."

"But his skin is all sweaty and shiny." He stopped his hands at his chin and stared at the beefy man still dancing to the techno music on the nearby platform. "And his G-string is so small. Ryker, don't make me do it."

"He's not making you do anything." Austen sipped her drink as she leaned back in the red armchair. "We're making you do it. You know if we'd lost, we'd be at Mickey's Topless Dancers right now."

Jared sighed. "They're right. Let's get this over with."

I wasn't as repulsed by the situation as I thought I might be. Austen seemed to always bring a smile to my face, so I found the situation comical. Besides, I was so secure in my masculinity and sexuality that I could touch a naked dude and still think about fucking Austen without any problems. "You'll be fine, Liam."

He leaned toward my ear and spoke over the music. "The things we do to get laid, huh?"

I left the couch and walked to the guy dancing right at our table. I grabbed a hundred bills and tucked them into the thin piece of string keeping his junk in check.

The stripper turned to me, wearing a grin. "Thanks, sexy."

Now I was a little grossed out, but I played along and gave him a thumbs-up before I returned to the table.

"You can't do that," Austen said. "You gave the guy all your cash."

I shrugged. "He earned it. You just said he's great with his hips."

Austen shook her head, but the irritated look in her eyes was forced. The playfulness still shone underneath.

The other guys shoved their cash inside the G-strings of the other dancers. Liam stood five feet away and leaned his body in the opposite direction as he tried to place the cash inside the man's underwear. He cringed and looked like he was about to vomit.

Madeline laughed. "Your brother is quite the character."

"He's a weirdo," Austen said. "A great brother, but also a weirdo."

"Jared seems to be doing alright." Jenn stirred her drink and watched their friend move around platforms, handing out cash like candy.

Instead of watching them, I turned back to Austen. Under the glow of the lights, she looked hypnotic. Even dressed in jeans and a t-shirt, she was sexy. I pictured her on her back on my bed, her legs wrapped around my waist. My thoughts got carried away with me, and I pictured her tits shaking every time I thrust into her. I pictured her the shape of her mouth as she moaned for me. Explicit thoughts rushed through my mind, and my cock was so hard in my jeans it was borderline uncomfortable.

Austen met my look, holding the straw of her drink in her hand. "What?"

I hadn't blinked in nearly a minute. I was absorbed in my fantasies, picturing the sweet sensations we would feel once our bodies were combined. My stare was obvious, and I quickly looked away. "I was looking at the dancer behind you."

"I sure hope not," Austen said. "Because that gaze was pretty intense."

I smiled but kept my eyes off her face. "What can I say? I'm an intense guy."

The guys continued to drain their cash by handing it out to the dancers on the floor. When they were finally finished, they came back to the seats, clearly relieved all the touching was over.

"I'm going to the bathroom to wash my hands," Liam said. "I don't want to accidentally touch myself later when a dude was the last thing I touched."

"Me too," Jared said. "My hands smell like money."

"I've gotta pee, so I'll hitch a ride." Jenn set her drink on the table.

Madeline followed behind her. "Make sure no one drops anything in my drink."

"You got it." Austen gave her a thumbs-up.

They left the table, leaving the two of us alone together.

She crossed her legs and stared at me, mirroring the intense look I just gave her a moment ago. The seats beside her had been vacated, and I moved so I could be closer to her. The music was loud overhead, and the only way we could hear each other was by yelling.

The second I was next to her, I felt the same heat I did last time.

She turned her head and stared at me, her lips red and her eye makeup dark. Her hair was curled, and I pictured the way it would look across my pillow as she lay underneath me, her legs wrapped around my waist. "In case you didn't notice, I was eye-fucking the shit out of you just now."

Heat seared all the way down my spine, from my neck down to my waist. When women were forward with me, I didn't always find it arousing. Sometimes, it seemed desperate. But in Austen's case, her confidence was the sexiest thing in the world. She had no problem saying what was on her mind. She didn't care about repercussions or rejection. She was immune to it. "How ironic. I was doing the same thing."

"So, we were eye-fucking just now? In front of everyone? That's pretty dirty." She leaned toward me like we were sharing a secret. Her perfume somehow entered my nose and took precedence over the stench of cheap booze and sweaty strippers.

"Or not dirty enough." She slipped her hand over mine on the armrest, her soft skin brushing against my knuckles. She came on to me with complete confidence, holding herself like a queen who deserved everything her heart desired.

Jesus Christ.

She interlocked our fingers and stared at me with her beautiful blue eyes that continued to fuck me where I sat. "I say we take off and head back to my place. I'm tired of all the looking and no touching."

My zipper was about to break because my cock was so hard. I wanted to press my mouth into the valley of her breasts and taste her everywhere. I wanted to dump a bottle of scotch on her skin and lick it up. I wanted to fuck her in every place she would allow me to.

My body reacted on its own, and my hand dug into her hair and pulled her face to mine. I crushed my mouth against hers and kissed her far too passionately for a public place. My mouth was on fire, but I loved the burn.

Her tongue darted into my mouth and danced with mine. Her warmth breath fell on my skin and made me come alive. My hand was still interlocked with hers, and I squeezed it as I kissed her harder. I pulled her bottom lip into my mouth and gave a slight bite.

When she bit me back, I knew she liked it.

While I was stuck in the moment with her, I knew everyone would be back at the table at any moment. And if Liam saw me making out with his sister, he wouldn't be too happy. I'd lost control, but now I had to get it back. I broke our kiss and pulled my mouth away, feeling the numbness in my lips. My mouth ached to be pressed against hers once more.

She grabbed the front of my shirt and yanked me back toward her, her mouth dangerously close to mine. "Let's get a cab."

I grabbed her hand and pulled it off my shirt even though I liked the way she gripped me. I could tell she would be awesome in the sack, wild and adventurous. Now I hated myself for ever befriending Liam in the first place. He was the biggest cockblock on the planet. "Austen, it's never going to happen."

She rolled her eyes so hard they nearly disappeared in the back of her head. "So you eye-fuck me then make out with me, but you're going to leave me hanging? I thought good men always finish the job."

"You seduced me, and you know it."

"Yeah? So what? When I want something, I take it. That's obviously not the case for you."

"Whoa, let's dial it down with the insults, okay?" I glanced over my shoulder to make sure everyone wasn't almost upon us. "I always take what I want. But Liam is my friend. There are rules about this sort of thing."

"I think rules are meant to be broken."

Could she be any more perfect?

"I've asked you out once, and I made my move. If it's not going to happen, then I'm going to move on. So, what's it going to be?"

I watched her lips move and yearned to kiss her once more. I wanted to steal her breath away and never give it back. "I slept with a friend's sister before, and it didn't end well. He and I aren't friends anymore, and she and I didn't work out. I learned my lesson."

She tilted her head to the side as she regarded me. "No two situations are alike, and you know that. But if you really don't want to go down this road, I respect that. But don't expect me to wait around. I'm not the kind of woman to wait for a guy to change his mind." Like she meant it literally, she left the chair and walked off, trailing into the shadows of the club and disappearing.

Chapter Four

It was ten in the morning when my phone rang on the nightstand.

I glanced at the screen and saw Rae's name.

I silenced it.

I had five voice mails from her that had accumulated over the past few weeks. I hadn't listened to a single one, knowing exactly what they would say. She would be worried about me, and she would be hurt that I didn't have the decency to take her calls after everything we'd been through.

I couldn't even text her back.

I didn't know what my problem was.

I finally got out of bed and did my routine. I hit the gym, made a protein shake, took a shower, and then sat in my living room and watched daytime TV. Last night, I went home alone and used my hand to exorcise all the sexual frustration bottled deep inside my chest. Austen was the object of my fantasy, those soft lips on my mouth and around my cock.

Goddammit, she was hot.

But I couldn't have her. I'd already crossed a line when I kissed her. I wasn't even sure how I managed not to go home with her last night.

Perhaps I was a better guy than I gave myself credit for.

John called me later in the afternoon, hitting me up to do something that night. I invited Liam along too since they were friends. Maybe we could pick up some women, and I could do my best to forget about Rae and Austen.

If Austen weren't Liam's sister, she would be the perfect distraction for me. I would think about Rae less and less as time went on. Getting lost in good sex with a beautiful woman was the perfect medicine. I did it when Rae and I broke up, and it helped for a long time—until everything collapsed around me.

We went to Strobe, a classy bar on Fifth. The buy-in just to walk inside was a hundred bucks a piece. Liam was strapped for cash because his music shop wasn't lucrative, so I paid his way in.

All the women were in skintight dresses and heels with beautiful hair and detailed makeup. They all looked great. But then again, the lights were low, and I was doing anything not to think about Austen.

We stood at the bar and ordered our drinks.

John clinked his glass against mine. "Sorry about your dad, man."

"Thanks." I swallowed the scotch, eager for the warmth to light my gullet on fire. "It's been almost a year now."

"How's your mom doing?" Liam asked.

"She was a wreck in the beginning." There wasn't a time when I looked at her and she wasn't sobbing. "But after a few months, it got easier. She's in a better place now, but she'll never be the same."

"She'll pull through," Liam asked. "Eventually."

"Your brother is still there?" John asked.

"Yeah, he took over COLLECT," I explained.

"So you hated it there, or what?" John asked. "You weren't there very long. I mean, I knew you didn't want to go to begin with, but I thought you would last longer than that."

Yes, I'd hated my job. But I needed a fresh start more than anything else. "It wasn't my cup of tea. My brother said he wanted to partner with me, so I just decided to bow out and give him the business."

"That was nice of you." John downed half his drink in a single gulp.

It was a perk for both of us. Money didn't mean anything to me when I had plenty of it. "What's new with you? Are you still seeing Leslie?"

"Nah." He shook his head but didn't seem sad about it. "Didn't work out."

"That's too bad," I said. "She was cute."

"Too jealous," he said. "Always looking through my phone and flipping out if I even hugged another woman. Got too much."

I never considered myself to be a jealous person until things started up with Rae. Every time Zeke was near her, I wasn't happy about it. I'd never been jealous before or after. "Sounds like too much work."

"I've never been the jealous type," Liam said. "When I'm with a woman, I know she's not gonna go looking for someone else. I'm just too sexy."

I shared a look with John and rolled my eyes.

John did the same.

"Dude, Madeline is damn hot." Liam rested his elbows on the bar as he stood beside me. "Those lips, that hair, that body...she's an angel. I'd give anything to watch her dance."

"You can always buy tickets to the ballet," I reminded him. "But that would make you a little bit of a stalker."

"Yeah, it would be creepy," Liam said in agreement.

"Why didn't you ask her out?" I asked. "Wasn't that the whole reason why we went bowling?"

"I've got to take my time, you know," Liam explained. "Play it cool."

I'd never played it cool in my life. And neither did Austen—apparently.

The subject changed to sports, which we talked about at great length. Sports was a great topic because it stole my focus and I didn't think about anything else. I didn't wonder what Rae was doing back in Seattle, and I didn't wonder if I made a mistake by not sleeping with Austen when I had the chance.

***

"Check out that babe." John brought his lips to his glass and nodded to a table on the other side of the room.

I turned around and glanced in the direction he indicated, seeing a brunette in a backless black dress. She stood at the table with her drink in front of her, which was halfway empty. I recognized that shiny hair and perfect body. Those legs had been in countless fantasies of mine.

It was Austen.

A guy walked over to the table in jeans and a black t-shirt. He was tall and handsome, with rugged features that reminded me of an old movie star. Just like her friend Jared, he was a good-looking guy.

She chuckled at something he said, and he got closer to her, close enough to suggest they were on a date.

The jealousy exploded out of nowhere. Like a volcano with an eruption that was long overdue, I burst into fiery flames and lava. My jaw tightened in disappointment, and I counted the inches that existed between them. I just saw Austen the other night, and she made good on her word.

She'd already landed another guy.

"Damn, she's with someone," John said with a sigh. "The good ones are always taken."

Liam returned from the bathroom and grabbed his whiskey from the counter. "What are you girls whispering about?"

"That hot chick over there," John said with a nod.

"Actually, she's not his type." I managed to unhinge my jaw long enough to say that.

"All women are my type," Liam argued. "Tall or short, it doesn't matter to me."

"Well, this one is your sister, so I think you'll feel otherwise." I pointed at the table where they were talking.

Liam narrowed his eyes until he recognized her face and brown hair. Then he stuck out his tongue in disgust. "Seven million people in this city but I run into her. Luck isn't on my side tonight. Let's head somewhere else."

I didn't want to walk away. If their date was going well, things might heat up and she could end up spending the night at his place. It shouldn't matter to me if that happened, but it didn't settle right with me. I wanted to take her home, not let some other guy enjoy her beautiful qualities. "I'm gonna stay here. There's this woman I've been eyeing, so I'm gonna go for it."

"You sure you don't want us to wait?" John asked.

"No, I'll catch up with you guys." I raised my glass to them. "Or better yet, I hope I don't."

After a chuckle, Liam and John walked out and continued their adventure.

I turned back to the bar and discreetly watched them together, seeing the way she smiled effortlessly. I was straight, but I knew a good-looking guy when I saw one. All he had to do was be a little charming, and he could seal the deal.

The idea just pissed me off more.

When their glasses were empty, he returned to the bar to order another round.

Without thinking twice about it, I walked right up to her table. I approached her from the side, so she didn't notice me right away. I was probably the last thing on her mind right now, the last guy she expected to see that evening.

When she noticed me in her peripheral, she glanced in my direction. She did a causal double take when she recognized me, assuming she must be mistaken. One eyebrow popped up before it returned to place. "Did you get lost on your way to the strip club?"

I admired how quick she was on her feet. Even when she was caught by surprise, she had a witty comment to break the ice. Her confidence was constant. Not even an earthquake could shake it. "Only if we're gonna make out again."

A soft smile spread across her lips, highlighting the rest of her beautiful features. "Small world, huh? Are you here with anyone?"

"Liam and my friend John. They just left."

She glanced at her date, who was still standing at the bar trying to get their drinks. "I should tell you, I'm kinda on a date right now."

I figured that out all by myself. "You don't waste any time, huh?"

She wore the same smile, the sparkle in her eyes. "I told you I'm not the kind of woman to wait around. Jason and I work together. He asked me out at the end of the day, and since I think he's cute, I figured it would be fine."

"You think it's smart to date someone you work with?"

She narrowed her eyes like I'd insulted her. "You think it's smart not to date someone just because you're friends with her brother?"

I smiled when she cornered me. "Touché."

She glanced at him again before she turned back to me. "Well, have a good night. Hopefully, I'll see you around."

I didn't want to walk away and let anything happen between him. But to purposely sabotage her date was a dick move. I had my chance, and I blew it—like always. "You want to come over and watch the game tomorrow night?"

Her brown hair was in soft curls that fell around her shoulders. Diamonds were in her ears, and a diamond pendant hung around her neck. She looked like a classy woman, but her own glow outshone every piece of jewelry she wore. Her complexion was perfect, just as fair as a collectible doll. Her eyes were bright and full of intelligent and ferocity. Everything about her was captivating—especially the words that came out of her mouth. "Correct me if I'm wrong, but that sounded like you just asked me on a date."

"I asked you to come over for a beer—and sex." I was going down a dangerous path, but I couldn't stop myself. I had this feisty woman on my hands, a woman harder than steel. I should have kept kissing her the other night and taken her home instead of waiting until now to make my move. Or better yet, I should have walked out with the guys instead of coming over here. I was at war with myself, unsure what to do. I didn't want to piss off Liam, but damn, I wanted to fuck this woman.

She shook her head with disappointment. "I'm gonna give it to you straight, Ryker. I think you're one of the hottest men I've ever seen in my life."

I grinned. "I like what I'm hearing."

"I wanted to jump your bones the second I laid eyes on you. You look like a man who knows how to work a headboard."

"Getting better."

"But I put my cards on the table. I told you what I wanted. I made my move." She moved closer to me and lowered her voice. "And you said you weren't interested."

"That's not what I said."

"Whatever. You turned me down. Now the only reason why you're over here is because you see that another man wants me. There's one thing I don't do—play games. I'm not the kind of woman to ditch a very nice guy just to run off with someone else. You had your chance, and you didn't take it."

I wanted to argue with her, but she put me in my place good. She told me what I deserved to hear. But damn, that made me want her more. I was attracted to her fire, her no-bullshit attitude. I wanted a woman so strong, so confident, that she could turn me down without thinking twice about it. "The only reason why I said no was because of your brother—and we both know that. Believe me, I'm just as interested in you now as I was when I first looked at you."

"That's a lame excuse, Ryker. Who gives a shit who my brother is? I'm a grown woman, and he's a grown man. Who I fuck is none of his concern. But if you aren't mature enough to understand that, it was never going to work anyway."

There wasn't enough time in the day to explain to her what happened with Rae. I didn't give a shit when she and I started seeing each other. I never cared that Rex was her brother. I didn't see why it mattered. But it made all the difference in the world. I had to remember not all siblings were the same, that Austen and Liam weren't nearly as close.

She saw that her date was returning, so she turned to me, a cold expression on her face. "I'll see you later, Ryker. Have a good night."

My instinct was to fight for her, but that would make me a bigger jerk. While I hated the guy she was out with it, he did nothing wrong. The only reason why I was in this situation was because I put myself there. "Yeah...you too."

Chapter Five

Rae left another message.

I didn't listen to it.

It'd been a month since I left Seattle, and I still didn't have the balls to talk to her. She was going to assume I left because of her—which wasn't untrue. The guilt was probably eating her alive, and she just wanted to know I was okay.

But I was still a dick.

I wasn't going to avoid her forever. Things didn't work out between us, but that didn't mean I hated her. I didn't want the erase the possibility of a friendship—someday. But right now, the sting was from her rejection was still too painful.

The last person I expected to text me sent me a message. *Call her back. She's worried about you.* It was my old friend, the man who won Rae. He would get to spend the rest of his life with her because he wasn't stupid like I was. I'd had Rae in my grasp, had her forever, and I threw her away.

I opened a beer and drank half of it before I finally had the courage to call her back. I stared at her name on the screen for a long time before my thumb finally hit the call button. I held the phone to my ear, and she picked up before it even rang.

"Ryker?" Just from saying my name, I could hear all her concern, all her desperation—everything. She inhaled a breath of relief even though she didn't hear me say a word. She was just grateful I called her back.

Wow. I'm such an ass. "Hey." I swallowed the lump in my throat, feeling all the pain from that night when she left me forever. I told her to go back to Zeke. After what he did, I didn't necessarily think he deserved her more than I did. But I could tell she was so madly in love with him that I would never compete. I would always be second best to a man she truly wanted. "I'm sorry I haven't called." I didn't make up an excuse about being too busy. We both knew what the real problem was.

"It's okay. I'm just glad I'm talking to you now." She breathed quietly over the phone like she was pacing, probably somewhere in Zeke's house with Safari watching her from his bed. "When I went to work and they said you stepped down…I was surprised."

That probably wasn't the best way for her to find out. "My brother wanted in, so I bowed out." Just like how I bowed out of our relationship. "There wasn't anything left for me in Seattle, so I moved back to Manhattan. I never gave up my apartment, so it's still here."

"Yeah, I figured that's where you went."

I drank my beer then pressed the cool glass to my temple. The silence filled the space between us, awkward and heavy. I knew this woman so well, but I didn't feel close to her at all. I felt like I lost a piece of myself when she left. "How are things with the gang?" I didn't ask about Zeke specifically. Honestly, I didn't really want to know.

"Good. Jessie is pregnant."

"Good for her. Is Tobias the lucky man?"

"Yep."

"Tell her congratulations for me."

"I will."

"And how's Rex...?" Probably happy I was gone and Zeke was back with his sister.

"He's the same—a dumbass."

An uncontrollable chuckle escaped my lips. "Some things never change, huh?"

"Nope. What about you? What's it like there?"

It didn't feel quite like home—at least not yet. "The same as I left it. I've been spending a lot of time with friends, going out and hitting the town."

"Uh-oh," she said. "I hope the NYPD can handle it."

I chuckled. "I've been behaving myself."

"Working anywhere?"

"No. I think I'm gonna retire for good."

"Sounds nice," she whispered. "Sometimes I think I could do it, but then I realize how bored I would be. I always have to be doing something. I've always been that way."

"You don't strike me as the stay-at-home type of person."

"No. Safari would drive me crazy if I were."

I laughed again. "But he would be happy."

Her breathing changed, making it seem like she was sitting rather than pacing. "So…any women in your life?"

The question was awkward, but it was bound to come up. It shouldn't be a taboo topic. She was with Zeke now, and I needed to move on with my life. We were friends—for the most part. "Not really. I met this one woman who's pretty cool. But I don't think it's going to go anywhere."

"Why not?"

"She's my friend's younger sister."

She laughed like I made a joke. "When has that ever stopped you before?"

An unwilling smile stretched my lips. "I don't want to go down that path again. A lot of drama."

"But I'm sure your friend isn't a weirdo like Rex. He and I are different from other families. We're freaks, and you know it."

Their relationship had annoyed me from time to time, but honestly, their closeness made me jealous once in a while. I was never close with my father or my brother. I talked to my mom, but there wasn't much of a connection there either. There was no bond. "Good freaks."

"I wouldn't let that stop you. If you like her, go for it."

"I waited too long to make a move. She told me I rejected her too many times and now she's looking for other fish in the sea."

"Damn," Rae said. "Sounds like a hardass."

"She is…but I think that's why I like her."

"You'll wear her down eventually. You've got the body for it."

I smiled at the compliment. "I hope it's enough for her."

She chuckled. "If she's straight, it'll definitely be enough. Trust me."

My chest relaxed now that the tension had disappeared. We were talking as friends—like we used to.

"Ryker?"

"Hmm?"

"I don't expect us to be best friends. But...maybe we can keep in touch?"

I gripped the empty beer in my hand and pictured her face while she spoke. I could practically see her standing right in front of me, those beautiful lips moving as her comforting words came out. "Yeah, I'd like that." I knew she still loved me. A part of her always would. But I feared I would always be in this place—being in love with the woman I couldn't have.

"Cool. Well, I'll talk to you later..."

"Alright. Tell the gang I said hi."

"I will. And you better not dodge my calls again, alright?"

My smile dropped when the guilt throbbed in my chest. "You got it."

***

"Take that, asshole." Liam hit the buttons on the controller and rammed his car into mine. My vehicle spun out and slammed into the pole on the side of the road. "While you get your tires fixed, I'm headed to the finish line."

I got my car back on the road and accelerated. I moved through the spaces between the other cars and caught up quicker than he expected. In the nick of time, I passed him and crossed the finish line, taking first place. "Now look who's the asshole?" I smacked the back of his head.

"Ouch." He ran his fingers through his hair and massaged the area where I just struck him. "Don't damage the goods, alright? This is gonna be worth a lot of money someday."

"Because scientists are going to want to study it to find the true definition of stupidity?"

He smacked me upside the head. "They already got their answer from you."

I turned off the game and flipped on the TV. "You're lucky I'm not going to kill you. I feel particularly generous today."

"Well, you're lucky I'm more of a pacifist."

"You mean, pussy."

"Hell no." Before he could get more into it, his phone rang. "Hey, Mom. What's up?"

I heard her voice come through the line. "Hello, dear. We're having a BBQ and wanted to see if you wanted to stop by. Your sister and her friend Madeline are here."

"Madeline?" he asked excitedly. "Hell yeah, I'll be there."

I smacked his arm and pointed at my chest.

"What?" he mouthed, having no idea what I was asking.

"Ask if I can come," I whispered. I didn't want to drop in on a family get-together, but if Austen was there, I wasn't going to pass up the opportunity.

"Oh." He turned back to the phone. "Can my friend Ryker come along too? We're hanging out right now."

"Of course," she said with excitement. "We have lots of food, so please come hungry."

"We will. See you soon, Mom."

"Bye, sweetheart."

He hung up and shoved his phone into his pocket. "I'm surprised you wanted to come."

"Well, think about it. I could distract Austen so you can be alone with Madeline." It was the perfect cover-up to my real intentions with Austen.

He bought it. He snapped his fingers then pointed at me. "That's a damn good plan."

"I'm very wise. I know."

"Let's head out and grab a six-pack on the way."

"Good idea."

Chapter Six

Austen

"How'd it go with Jason?" Madeline sat across from me at the picnic table. She sipped a glass of water with a slice of lemon wedged on the side of the plastic cup. Being a ballerina was tough work. She had to eat nothing to stay thin, but yet, she had to pull some insane stunts without any carbs.

I could never do it.

"It was okay. We went out for a few drinks then he took me home."

"Anything good happen there?"

My parents were inside the house preparing the burgers and condiments. We were out of earshot so I could discuss the intimacy of my sex life. "He kissed me good night, but that was it."

She propped her chin on her hand. "Didn't feel anything?"

I thought he was hot, but my libido went out the window when Ryker made an appearance. He was the sexiest man I'd ever laid eyes on, and thinking about him made me forget about Jason completely. I didn't invite Jason inside because I wished it were Ryker taking me home instead. Something about that guy made my thighs squeeze together. I'd killed the battery to my vibrator last night because I'd been using it so much since I met him.

Of course, I didn't tell Madeline any of this.

We were close. But not that close.

"Guess not." I sipped my Corona and enjoyed the shade the tree provided. I was used to the humid summers on the East Coast. When the sun was nearly gone and the temperature started to cool, it was my favorite time of the year.

"I'm guessing Ryker is off the table?" She grabbed the lemon off her glass and squeezed the juice into her water. When the peel was destroyed, she tossed it inside where it floated on top of the ice.

"Yeah. I made my move, and he turned me down. So that's over." I'd been rejected before. What woman hadn't? But it didn't shake my confidence or deter me from asking out another guy, if I ever saw one that caught my attention. But if he wasn't into it from the beginning, I moved on to something else. I wasn't the kind of woman who chased a guy. Too much self-respect for that.

"Is he a freak or something?"

"He said it was because of Liam. Since they're friends and all." I rolled my eyes. "But when he saw me with Jason the other night, he made a pass at me."

"So, he is interested in you?"

"Not really," I explained. "I think that drop-dead gorgeous god is used to women obsessing over him and waiting around for him to call. So when he realized I wasn't into that stupidity, it made him question just how sexy he really is. I think that's what lit a fire under his ass."

"Possibly," she said. "Or maybe he was just jealous."

"Who knows?" I grabbed a chip and dunked it into the sweet onion dip. "Doesn't matter anyway. There are plenty of fish in the sea, right?"

"Uh...I don't know about that." Her gold earrings dangled from her lobes and reflected the sun with every little move she made. "Ryker is pretty damn delicious. If that guy said he was on *GQ* this month, I would believe him—in a heartbeat."

"Yeah...he does look tasty."

"If you didn't call dibs on him, I would have gone for him."

"I don't have dibs anymore, so he's all yours."

She eyed the chip bowl but didn't dare take one. "Honestly, I think your brother is kinda cute."

"Really?" I couldn't help but make a disgusted face. I loved my brother because he was the best guy I knew with a heart of gold, but I would never forget the experience of sharing a bathroom with him. There were some memories that just couldn't be erased no matter how hard I tried.

"Okay, I think he's really cute," she said with a laugh. "But is that weird for you?"

It would be pretty hypocritical if I said it was. "Just don't stick your tongue down his throat in front of me, and we're good."

"Because I've done that before," she said sarcastically.

"I'm just saying..." I dunked another chip into the dressing and popped it into my mouth. There was nothing better than chips and dip on a hot summer day.

My dad walked into the backyard with the burgers wrapped in foil. He got the grill going while holding a beer in one hand, refusing to put it down for even a second. Mom's voice carried through the screen door in the house.

"Liam must be here," I said. "Here's your chance to make something happen."

"We'll see how it goes," she said. "I can't really tell what kind of—"

I grabbed another chip and dunked it into the dip, getting over half of it submerged before I shoved it into my mouth. "Hmm?" I didn't know why she'd stopped speaking so abruptly because I was so focused on eating.

She kept eyeing the back door. "Ryker is here."

I hid my expression so no one would notice my surprise. A sudden thrill jolted through me, followed by the blush in my cheeks and the tightness of my thighs. But after I took a breath, all those emotions passed. He may be the sexiest hunk I'd ever seen, but he was still just a dude. I wasn't going to let him get me worked up.

Liam reached the table first, his eyes on Madeline like I didn't exist. "Long time, no see."

"Hey." Madeline kept her cool so well I couldn't tell she was attracted to my brother. "You got here just in time. There are still chips left."

"Phew." Liam helped himself to the seat beside her. "I'm glad Austen didn't eat them. She tends to do that."

I ignored the insult because Ryker immediately took the seat beside me, his arm brushing against mine because he didn't leave any space between us. The hard muscles of his arms grazed against my soft skin, making me think of the countless fantasies I had about him. I was a big fan of arm porn. You know, the kind that's chiseled to perfection and you just can't stop staring.

Ryker had those kinds of arms.

"Hey, Stone Cold." His flirty tone passed over me like his fingertips were directly on my skin.

I refused to call him by the name I'd given him. "Hey. Chips and dip?"

"No thanks. I'll wait until the burgers are ready."

Liam got cozy with Madeline and asked her how dance recital was the night before. They fell into quiet conversation together, Madeline still keeping her cool about her attraction.

That left me to fend for myself against Ryker. The spell of pine and bar soap came over my nose just the way it did the last time I was this close to him. When he kissed me, my toes curled in my shoes until they ached, and my lips trembled like an electric current passed through them. Everything about him reeked of sex—good sex. When he turned me down twice, it didn't hurt my confidence, but trust me, I was disappointed.

"So, how'd your date go?" He rested his elbows on the wooden table as he leaned close to me. He didn't seem to care if Liam noticed our proximity because he only came closer and closer.

"Fine." I wasn't giving him more than that.

"Are you going to see him again?"

"Maybe." No, I wasn't. I didn't like him enough to risk an awkward work relationship. But I didn't want to put all my cards on the table for Ryker to see. I'd already done that before, so he lost his privileges.

"Did you kiss him?"

I popped a chip into my mouth and took my time chewing it, drawing out the pause as long as possible.

His eyes were glued to my face, dark and intense.

"I'm not really a kiss-and-tell kind of lady."

Ryker somehow figured out the answer from that response. "Nothing compared to what we had, huh?"

The arrogant comment ruffled my feathers, but it did nothing to douse my attraction.

"Come over after dinner."

"I'm good."

He narrowed his eyes, but my response seemed to excite him more. "We can play this cat-and-mouse game all you want, but you know what happens at the end."

"The cat gets his paw stuck in a mousetrap?"

He smiled with his lips but not his eyes. "The cat gets what he wants." His green eyes were scorching and brilliant, drilling right into me like he could see past my front. His wide shoulders looked perfect for gripping, and those soft lips looked perfect for kissing. I wanted that hot body on top of mine, covered in sweat as he shoved his impressive length inside me. I hadn't had a good lay in a while, and I was losing my mind.

Can you tell?

***

After dinner, we said goodbye to my parents then walked to the street. I usually walked home instead of taking a cab because I preferred the exercise. At work, I sat at a desk all day and didn't get to stretch my legs very often.

Liam and Madeline shared a cab because they both lived in the same direction.

So that left me alone...with him.

"Can I walk you home?" He walked beside me, his hands in his front pockets. The t-shirt fit his sculpted body well, showing his powerful chest and shoulders. He had long legs, and I assumed he had muscled thighs just the way I liked.

"I can manage." I was never afraid to walk the city at night. I had my pepper spray and my fist to take out anyone who crossed me. If a guy tried to rob me, he'd be collapsed on the ground with a broken dick.

"Well, how about you walk me home?" He came close to me, his arm nudging me gently in the side. "I could use the company."

I smiled at his sly move. "You seem like you can manage."

His arm snaked around my waist, and he pulled me tighter into his side. His strong core pressed against me, feeling like concrete rather than a person. His face leaned toward mine, his five o'clock shadow brushing against my skin. "I don't want to jerk off tonight—unless it's on your tits." He maneuvered me until my back hit the wall of a building we were passing. I didn't even notice it because I was absorbed in his intense gaze and sexy mouth.

He pressed his body into mine and dug one hand into my hair. He fisted it like he owned me, like I was his property to do with whatever he wished. He hiked up my leg around his and kissed me hard on the mouth, taking my breath away with his intensity.

The outline of his cock was defined in his jeans, and he pressed it right against my clit, giving me the most exquisite friction I'd ever felt in my life. He pulled my bottom lip into his mouth and gave it a gentle bite before he kissed me with his sexy embrace.

I knew he was trying to seduce me to get me in naked in his bed.

And it was working.

It was working really well.

He rubbed against me as he kept kissing me, making me feel like the sexiest woman in the world. He was a phenomenal kisser, the kind I would never forget as long as I lived. It made my kiss with Jason feel like an embrace between two cousins. It wasn't full of the raw passion we shared now.

He gave me his tongue and moaned with me, enjoying every touch and caress as much as I did. His hard length continued to press against me, pushing me further into oblivion. He had me on the precipice of ecstasy but didn't push me over the edge. He kept me right there with him, torturing both of us.

Now I didn't care about going back on my word. I didn't care that he rejected me before. I knew Ryker was a golden ticket, a guaranteed night of unbelievable sex that would blow my mind and curl my toes.

So I was going for it. "Let's go to your place." I gripped his biceps and pulled his body farther into mine, memorizing the feel of his length against me. I could count the inches and measure the girth by the pressure he applied against my clit. I wanted that cock everywhere—in my mouth and between my legs.

He kept his mouth pressed against mine. "Can you wait that long, sweetheart?"

If he fucked me against this wall, I probably wouldn't stop him. "No. So we should hurry."

***

Once the door opened, our mouths were glued together once more. He kicked the door shut with his foot then lifted me into the air until my legs were secured around his waist. My hands dug into his soft hair as we kissed down the hallway and into his bedroom.

I didn't see a single piece of furniture in his apartment. Everything could be made of solid gold, and I still wouldn't give a damn. All I cared about was his bed—and getting fucked on it.

He lay me back on the foot of the bed and slipped my sandals off before he worked my jeans and got them off.

I shoved my panties off because we weren't moving quickly enough. I didn't need any foreplay because we'd been eye-fucking since the day we met. I was wet and good to go. His cock would have no problem sliding in and out no matter how big it was.

I didn't bother with my top because I just wanted him inside me. I wanted to feel every inch of his manliness. I wanted to feel that exquisite stretching that I missed so dearly. "Goddammit, get your clothes off."

The corner of his mouth rose in a smile as he yanked his shirt over his head. Like I pictured, he was all muscle—all man. He had perfectly outlined pecs, a chiseled stomach with a noticeable V between his hips, and the sexiest arms ever.

"Damn…" I licked my lips automatically, my eagerness driving me forward.

"You haven't seen anything yet, sweetheart." He undid his jeans and kicked them to his ankles. He stood in his boxers, his cock outlined by the fabric. He grabbed the band and teased me, slowly pulling it down.

I propped myself on my elbows and waited for the grand finale.

He yanked them off, letting his enormous cock pop out. Nine inches of female fantasy, he was long and hard as rock. His tip was darker than the rest of his length, swollen with erotic blood. A drop of lubrication had formed at the head, and my tongue wanted to lick it away.

"Jesus Christ."

His grin dropped, the intense gaze returning to his look. His look was so dark he nearly looked brooding. He grabbed a condom from the pocket of his jeans and slowly rolled it on, leaving a good gap at the tip for all the come he was about to deposit.

He pressed his thumb against my clit and rubbed me aggressively, making my legs spasm at his touch.

I let out an involuntary moan, already so horny that he didn't even need to touch me.

He slipped two fingers inside me and felt my slickness. "Fuck…that tight little cunt is ready for me."

"Yes…fuck me." I hadn't been this aroused in my life. I'd had good sex with amazing men, but nothing. I already wanted to come, and we hadn't even begun.

He grabbed my hips and dragged me until I was positioned perfectly at the edge of the bed. My ass hung off slightly, and he gripped me by the back of the knees, keeping my thighs far apart.

Like his cock had a mind of its own, his head found my entrance and slowly slid inside, moving through my mounds of lubrication and into my tight channel. He locked his eyes to mine and moaned. "Fuck, your pussy is amazing." He continued to inch all the way inside until he was completely sheathed.

I gripped his forearms and moaned with pure pleasure. His girth stretched me wide apart, slightly painful but so exquisite. He was so far within me that he nearly hit my cervix, just inches away. I never cared about size, but now that I'd been with a man with an enormous cock, I realized it mattered.

It mattered a lot.

"Shit, I'm gonna come already."

He slowly pulled out of me before he thrust back in. "I'm gonna make you come a lot tonight, sweetheart. So pace yourself."

I dug my nails into his forearms. "God...you're my hero."

He thrust his hips and fucked me hard, driving his cock forcefully into me and shaking my entire body with every movement. My tits moved with every thrust he gave, my nipples hard and pointed to the ceiling.

I gripped my tits and played with them, twisting my own nipples for him to enjoy. He ignited a heathen within me, turning me into sexual deviant that couldn't be satisfied. I didn't feel an ounce of hesitation for the things I was doing. I fell into him, into the moment, and didn't think about anything else.

"I want you to count with me." He leaned forward over the bed, driving his cock hard inside me as far as it would go, hitting me in the cervix and rubbing his pelvic bone against my clit.

As he expected, the fire erupted deep in my belly and stretched everywhere. My pussy clenched around him, and a scream exploded from my throat. I was consumed in volcanic fire, all the sensations hitting me at once. I came harder than I ever had in my life, his enormous cock still pounding into me. "God…yes."

He spoke with more authority than a war general. "Count."

I felt the high slowly recede from my body, but the tenderness remained behind. "One…"

***

It was around five in the morning when he positioned himself behind me and fisted my hair like reins on a horse. He yanked my head back and shoved himself inside me, feeling the same amount of wetness as he did hours ago.

"Oh…" I felt his cock slam into me, hitting the sweet spot almost instantly.

He gripped one of my hips and thrust into me like my pussy was his property. He worked his hips vigorously, our skin tapping together as we screwed like animals in spring. He grunted as he pumped into me, sweat covering his body as he worked to give it to me good.

This was heaven.

Ryker was a god made just to please women.

I was so grateful I got to be one of them.

He yanked my head back harder as he rammed his enormous dick inside me. "Your pussy is so fucking tight."

"You cock is just big."

He released my hair and grabbed my neck instead, squeezing me gently as he quickened his pace.

I felt the explosion between my legs. I gushed around his cock as my body soared into oblivion. The sensation was so exquisite that I couldn't appreciate it enough. It was so profound that my mind couldn't wrap around what I was experiencing. I gripped his wrist as his hand remained glued to my neck, screaming his name over and over.

Ryker pressed his lips to my ear, his hot breaths loud. "So. Fucking. Good." He released inside me with a moan, filling the condom as I finished my orgasm. His hand tightened on my neck until I could barely breathe, but I allowed it since I knew it would pass.

When I finished, my arms were shaking from the adrenaline still in my body. His hand loosened on my throat, and I finally inhaled a deep breath.

"Count." He kept his softening dick inside me, waiting for the number he wanted to hear me say out loud.

"Five…"

He pulled out and walked into the bathroom to toss the used condom in the garbage.

I collapsed on his sheets, more satisfied than I'd been in my entire life. No man had ever pleased me so thoroughly. My vibrator couldn't compete with that experience. I wasn't even sure if I should bother keeping it now that I'd been with Ryker.

I wanted to fall asleep in his luxurious bed, but it was almost six and I needed to get ready for work anyway. I lost an entire night of sleep, but it was totally worth it. I'd do it again in a heartbeat.

I got dressed in the clothes I arrived in and pulled on my panties even though they were still wet from earlier that evening. Instead of walking to my apartment, I would just fork over the cash to get a cab so I could avoid the walk of shame.

I grabbed my purse just when Ryker stepped out of the bathroom. He pulled on his sweatpants and looked at my fully clothed figure. "Heading out?"

"Yep. Unfortunately, I have work."

"Damn. Thought we could have another round."

I was thoroughly satisfied, but my thighs still tightened together in response. This man turned me into a puddle of hormones. "Maybe another time."

He walked me to the door, looking delicious shirtless. His hair was messy from my fingers running through it, and he had a sleepy look in his eyes. I wondered what he looked like first thing in the morning, but I didn't have to think for long. He was probably drop-dead gorgeous—like always.

"Last night was phenomenal." I hooked my arms around his neck and gave him a slow kiss. "You know how to show a woman a good time."

His arms wrapped around my waist, and he smiled against my lips. "And I didn't even take you to dinner."

"Who needs dinner when you can skip straight to dessert?" I kissed him on the cheek before I walked through the open door. "I'll see you around. I almost feel like I should leave a tip or something."

He leaned against the doorframe and chuckled. "You already tipped me good enough, sweetheart."

Before I blushed and jumped his bones again, I walked away. "Bye."

His deep voice followed me down the hallway. "Bye, Stone Cold."

***

I threw my clutch on the table before I hopped into the chair. "Stop whatever you guys are talking about. I have news—big news."

"Did you get a raise?" Jared asked.

"Already?" Jenn asked. "Nah. Did you fix the garbage disposal in your apartment?"

"No." I rolled my eyes. "Bigger than that."

"Did Ryker make a move last night?" Madeline asked.

"Bingo." I pointed at Madeline. "He made a move, and I took the bait." I told them the whole story, going into limited details about the sex. I didn't feel awkward telling them about my personal life since I told them everything.

"Wow." Madeline shook her head in disbelief. "He sounds too good to be true."

"I know," I said. "He's absolutely perfect."

"Are you gonna break your rule?" Jenn asked.

I never broke my rule—for any reason. It didn't matter how handsome, charming, or nice he seemed. I made this oath years ago, and I was sticking to it. But after being with Ryker, my foundation had been shaken. "I'm thinking about it..."

"Oh, damn," Jenn said. "Then he must be really incredible in the sack."

"Like you wouldn't believe." I waved down the bartender and got a beer. "A few more times wouldn't hurt, right? And he'd be down with it, I'm sure."

"He would," Jared said without hesitation. "You don't need to worry about that."

"What does this mean for Liam?" Madeline asked. "Since they're friends and all."

I shrugged. "I don't care. I don't even see why he would know about it—unless Ryker is an idiot."

"He could be," Jenn said. "Guys aren't that pretty unless they're stupid."

"True," Madeline said. "Liam is really hot, but he seems a little empty-headed sometimes."

I ignored the disgusting comment but not the insult. "Yeah, he's not the sharpest tool in the shed."

Chapter Seven

Ryker

That was one of the best lays I'd ever had.

And that was saying something because I fucked Rae for months.

Austen wasn't ashamed of her sexuality, of her carnal desires. She played with her tits while I fucked her. She even touched her asshole a little bit when I fucked her from behind. She was wild and unbridled, exactly my kind of flavor.

I wanted to fuck her again.

I didn't think of the repercussions of my actions until a few days later. I hoped she didn't assume we were in some kind of relationship. She didn't seem like the clingy type, but women were unpredictable sometimes. I wasn't looking for commitment because I was never going to be in another relationship—ever. It was all meaningless fucking from here on out.

When she didn't contact me for a few days, it seemed like the hookup was pretty casual. Unless she was waiting for me to call her. But then again, she didn't wait around for anyone, so if she wanted to talk, she would have made it happen.

I went out to lunch with Liam, getting a burger at Mega Shake. I'd been to the one in Seattle as well, and the two locations looked exactly the same. We got our food and took a seat in one of the booths.

"Anything happen with Madeline?"

"Nah. I took her home the other night, and that was it."

I gave him an incredulous look. "What the hell are you doing? If you wait too long, you're going to end up in the friend zone."

"I know what I'm doing, alright? I get pussy as much as you do."

I found that hard to believe. "If you don't make your move soon, someone else will. Just keep that in mind." When I didn't go for Austen, she went out with some other guy. It didn't seem like she'd slept with him, but there was no way for me to know.

"Women are like wine. You've got age them for a little bit."

I took a bite of my burger then washed it down with a drink of my soda.

"Was my sister annoying?"

I didn't understand the question, so I just stared at him. She definitely wasn't annoying during the five times I fucked her, not even a little bit. And even when we weren't fucking, she was pretty cool. "Sorry?"

"When you were distracting her at my folks' place."

"Oh…she was fine. She's pretty cool, actually."

"Yeah, she can be fun. We used to fight a lot when we were younger, but she turned out to be pretty awesome. I give her a hard time every once in a while, just to keep her grounded. Nothing worse than your sibling knowing you actually like them."

I chuckled. "That's why you were dodging her calls? Just to keep her on her toes?"

He shrugged. "I guess a little."

I laughed because it was a little ridiculous. "She's got a great sense of humor, and she's damn smart. She's one of the coolest chicks I've ever met." I grabbed a handful of fries and tossed them into my mouth.

Liam stared at me, his expression slowly hardening.

"What?"

"You have a thing for my sister?"

Did I just walk right into that? "Just because I think she's cool, I must be into her?"

"Well, every friend I've had has been into my sister. I'm used to it."

Did that mean he was cool with it? "Well, I'm not gay. Obviously, I think she's cute."

"Does that mean you're going to go for her?"

He didn't sound angry, which was strange. Rex wanted to murder me just for looking at Rae. "I don't see myself dating her, if that's what you're asking. But I'm definitely attracted to her." I would never tell Liam I hooked up with her. That was just an awkward conversation he didn't want to have.

"Good," he said with obvious relief. He took an enormous bite of his hamburger then went straight for his milk shake. "Then I don't need to warn you about her."

"Warn me about her...?" I couldn't tell how he meant that. Was he warning me to stay away from her? Or was he warning her to stay away from me? With Rex, his opinions were perfectly clear. Liam's view on his sister was completely different, probably because their parents were still in the picture. "What's that supposed to mean?"

"Never mind. If you aren't into her, then it really doesn't matter." He sipped his milk shake again. He covered his mouth when he couldn't hold back a belch.

The more he downplayed it, the more interested I became. "Liam, what do you mean? Does she have some kind of problem or something?"

"No, she doesn't have a problem," he said quickly. "She just has this reputation for being a bit of a heartbreaker."

Heartbreaker?

"I've never seen her with the same guy twice, and she flat out told my parents she was never getting married or having kids. I'm not sure what her philosophy is because I've never really talked about her it with her, but she's not the relationship kind of woman. She does her own thing."

When I looked back on our encounters, his description of her made sense. She hit on me and said exactly what she wanted. When she didn't get it, she moved on. She was a sexual creature who loved the sex but not the emotion.

It sounded too good to be true.

"So if you're looking for a relationship, steer clear." He drank his milk shake again before he turned back to his food. Whenever he ate, he always made a mess and got crap all over his face.

I normally told him about the stains, but this time I didn't bother. All I could think about was Austen and the fact that I just hit the jackpot. She and I were exactly the same—all sex and no commitment.

It couldn't be more perfect.

***

I called her when I got home. "Hey, Stone Cold."

"Hey, Sexy." A flirtatious tone was in her voice, the same one I heard when she left my apartment earlier that week. "What can I do for you?"

"I want to take you out to dinner—and dessert."

"Right to the chase," she said with a smile. "I like that."

And I really liked her.

"But I'm gonna have to pass. Thanks for the offer."

The cold rejection swept over me like an ocean tide. I was so excited to talk to her, but our relationship flopped like we hadn't just had incredible sex a few days ago. "Tomorrow night?"

"I have plans."

"And the following night…?" I was chasing her again even though I'd already been chasing her for weeks.

"Let's just say I'm busy for the indefinite future, Ryker. But I'm flattered. I'll see you around, okay?"

"Whoa, wait—"

Click.

Did she just hang up on me?

I called her back and listened to it ring twice before she answered.

"What's up?" she asked.

"Why are you blowing me off right now?" I couldn't keep the anger out of my voice because it was uncontrollable. I'd never slept with a woman and then gotten this kind of reaction. I knew I was awesome in bed, so that wasn't the problem.

"I'm not blowing you off," she said calmly. "I'm just not interested in dating you, Ryker. Obviously, I think you're smoking hot and the sex is amazing, but that's over. I don't do back-to-backs. Not my thing."

Was this how I talked to countless women before Rae came along? Man, I was an ass. "I don't want to date you either, Austen. But you bet your ass I want to fuck you again. And I know you want to fuck me. So let's sit down and have a conversation about it." She wounded my pride when she pushed me away, but that only made me want her more. The sex was too good for me to walk away without a fight. Why would I go out and pick up someone else when I could have amazing and meaningless sex with Austen?

"A conversation about fucking, huh? I still don't do back-to-backs."

Damn, Liam wasn't kidding. She really was a hardass. "I got the impression we were friends. You can't have dinner with a friend?"

She sighed into the phone when she understood this pursuit wasn't going to go away. "Yeah, sure. You want to meet at the Frog's Tooth?"

That wasn't the best place for a date, but I suspected she did that on purpose. "I'll see you at seven."

***

She walked inside in jean shorts and a blue tank top. The outfit was plain, but her body was so sexy she could rock anything and still look like a million bucks. Her hair was in a sleek ponytail, and she wore sandals.

On top of her looking hot as hell, she always looked cute.

She found me sitting in a booth and walked over to join me, her hips swaying as she walked. She slid into the booth beside me and didn't waste any time waving down a waitress and ordering a Long Island Iced Tea.

When I looked at her, I couldn't stop thinking about how sexy she looked underneath me. My cock still remembered exactly how her pussy felt, even through the condom. Every kiss and every touch were explosive. This woman knew her way around the bedroom as much as I did. "I like your hair." I would love to grab her by the ponytail and force her face into my lap, shoving my entire length down the back of her throat.

This woman must have read my mind because she smiled and said, "I'm sure you do." She took a long sip of her iced tea and didn't cringe at the liquor. "So, here I am. Fire away." She leaned against the back of the booth and stared me down like an executive in the boardroom. She had a natural feistiness to her that just made me more desperate to fuck her again.

"Why don't you do back-to-backs?"

"I don't like it," she said immediately. "The more time you spend with someone, a connection forms. And once that connection is there, the sex is less meaningless. And when that happens, the sex goes to shit."

I used to feel that way until I fell headfirst for Rae. Then the sex turned explosive. "I don't agree, but I see what you mean."

"So it's nothing personal, Ryker. You really are the best sex I've ever had. I just don't want to go down that road with you."

"What road?"

"You know, we start hooking up, and then feelings start to happen… I'm not looking for that."

"What a coincidence," I said with a smile. "Neither am I. Looks like we're on the same page."

"Perhaps." She sipped her drink again.

She was always honest, so I thought that would be the best tactic to get what I wanted. "You're one of the best lays I've ever had. Honestly, I don't want to stop. I could go out and find another woman, but I'd just be thinking about you anyway. So, how about we set something up?"

"Like what?" she asked. "A booty call?"

"Exactly. Only sex—no strings attached."

"Hmm…" She crossed her arms over her chest and leaned back against the seat. "I don't know."

She didn't know? After I made her come five times in one night, she wasn't sure? Was she playing games with me? Playing hard to get? "What's your hesitance?"

"People say that all the time—no strings attached. But it always gets messy. It always gets complicated. I don't think two people can have sex over and over and not feel something. I really wouldn't want to put you in that situation and hurt you."

I grinned because her concern was hilarious. "I think you're awesome, Austen. But I'm not gonna fall for you. You can count on that."

"You sound awfully confident." She cocked her head to the side, and she stared me down.

"Are you confident you won't fall for me?"

"Absolutely." She spoke without hesitation, like she already knew her answer before I even asked the question.

"If we both feel that way, there shouldn't be any problems." I drank my beer as I watched her, wishing we could have this conversation while my cock was impaled deep inside her.

She sipped her Long Island Iced Tea a few times as she considered the offer. She licked her lips then pressed them together, her eyes gaze turned out the window to the world beyond. "I'm not saying I'm agreeing to this, but if I were, what would be the ground rules?"

"Whatever you want them to be." I couldn't care less what parameters she wanted to have.

"Then we aren't exclusive."

A tinge of jealousy ripped through me out of nowhere. I could ask her to come over, but she could already be booked up for the night with some other guy. I wasn't a big fan of that, even though I wasn't sure why. "That's fine with me. But you might want to reconsider it."

"Why would I do that?"

"If we're sleeping with other people, we have to keep using protection. I prefer to fuck without a rubber. Monogamy has its perks."

She held my look with her lips pressed tightly together. "I don't do monogamy."

I felt like I was talking to myself—but with a vagina. Her need for freedom and lack of commitment mirrored my own philosophy. She was an independent woman who didn't need a man for anything. She had an impressive job, education, and a great head on her shoulders. She was beautiful and refused to settle for anything less than what she deserved. How could any man win over a woman who didn't need anyone but herself?

Fuck, that was hot.

Rae was independent too…but not this extreme.

"Then we won't be exclusive." Even with a condom, she still felt incredible. I'm sure she would give amazing head, so that would be enough for me. "Anything else?"

"Secrecy. I don't want you talking to my brother about us."

"Done." I wasn't going to do that anyway.

"If we can hang out together, we have to pretend nothing is happening between us. If I bring a date, you can't be weird about it."

"Done." I wasn't sure how well I would swallow that, but I could put on a brave face if I had to. "I have a request of my own."

"I'm listening."

"I want to be friends."

She raised an eyebrow like the question was perverse.

"I think you're a cool chick, and I like hanging out with you. I want us to be friends. I want the type of relationship where we can relax around one another, be honest with each other. We can get dinner together from time to time, and it's not questionable."

When she was silent, it wasn't obvious how she felt about that. She looked out the window again as she considered it. "I guess that would okay. As long as we understand what this is from the beginning, everything should be fine."

I nodded in agreement.

"No sleepovers."

I liked morning sex, so that was a pity. "Why?"

"I don't need to give a reason why. I just don't do sleepovers." When she was questioned, that's when the claws came out.

If someone asked me the same question, I'd probably have the exact same response. I'd never been particular about the women I was attracted to. There weren't any qualities that I preferred over others. But her badass, no-bullshit vibe was a serious turn-on. "Okay."

"Anything else?" she asked. "Are you into special kinks?"

I raised an eyebrow. "Why? Would you be willing to do them?"

"Of course. I've got my own fantasies I expect you to fulfill."

Instantly, I was hard in my jeans. I wanted to throw my drink on her chest and lick away every drop of my beer. "Good to know."

She brought her glass to her lips and took a drink, her curled brown hair begging to be touched.

I tossed more than enough cash on the table to cover our drinks. "Let's get out of here."

"Are we having a booty call already?" she asked as she licked her lips.

"Don't act like you don't wish we were fucking right now."

***

I loved her tits.

Perky. Firm. Round.

They were petite because she was a thin woman, but their perkiness made up for what she lacked in size. I cherished her soft skin and sucked her nipples hard into my mouth. I ravished her with my tongue, exploring her perfect body and the wonderful curves she possessed.

I was on top, her ankles hooked together in the center of my back. I thrust her frame into the mattress, tapping the headboard against the wall as I rocked my hips and fucked her good and hard.

She was soaking wet.

She breathed with me, her chest covered with sweat. Her nails dug into my shoulders and slowly trailed down my back, nearly cutting into my skin. She moaned as she took my cock over and over. "Ryker..." Her eyes lit up like fireworks as she whispered my name. She was so sexy without even trying, moving in the perfect ways to make me feel amazing.

I could stay buried inside her like this for the rest of time. Sex was incredible, but good sex like this made me feel alive. Feeling so good because of another person was electrifying. Her pussy was made just for my cock. "I'm gonna come, sweetheart." I'd pleased her enough, and now it was my turn.

She grabbed my ass and pulled me hard inside her. "Give it to me..."

I moaned as my cock twitched inside her. She wanted to watch me come because she found it arousing, and that just heightened my own pleasure. I pumped into her hard, nearly breaking my headboard because I was rocking with such intensity.

"Hold on."

My shaft was about to explode. I couldn't hold on any longer.

She rolled me onto my back then balanced on the balls of her feet. With her hands gripping my shoulders, she bounced down my length repeatedly. She had to pull herself high off the bed to reach my tip before she sheathed me to my balls once more. She grabbed my hands and placed them on her tits as she continued to move up and down. Fiery confidence was bright in her eyes, knowing she was making me feel like a king. "Now I want you to come."

She didn't need to tell me twice. My cock was throbbing with desperation as it ached to release into the tip of the condom. "Fuck, sweetheart."

She bounced on my dick harder, bringing me to the finish line with explosive energy. Her tits shook in my hands as she moved, her nipples hard like diamonds.

I released with a loud moan, exploding inside the condom with my eyes on her tits. My head rolled back as I enjoyed the delectable release, feeling the pleasure spread across my entire body. It was scorching hot. "Fuck..." The orgasm seemed to last forever, dragging on until it finally came to an end. When I didn't have an orgasm for a prolonged period of time, the next time I did, it was usually epic. But I just got laid a few days ago, and the pleasure was just as explosive now as it was then.

Because her pussy was that perfect.

Chapter Eight

Austen

When the workday was over, I walked out of the building and headed toward 2nd Street. Madeline and I were meeting at our favorite bakery, The Muffin Girl. Anytime we had an excuse to go there, we seized it.

She already had a table outside on the small terrace. Two creamy Frappuccinos sat there with our favorite carrot cake cupcakes. "I got the last two. Made a little girl cry, but it was worth it."

"When it comes to war, there will always be casualties."

"I'm glad you understand." She set a fork on my napkin, knowing I ate my cupcake the lame way. "How was work?"

"It was good. My eyes hurt from staring at a screen so long, but other than that, it was pretty normal."

"Run into Jason?"

"Yeah, but I told him it wasn't going to work."

"How'd he take it?" She scooped a piece of the cake and popped it into her mouth.

"He understood. It wasn't a big conversation." Jason worked in the IT department, so he was pretty laid-back. He didn't seem like the kind of guy who had temper issues.

"What about Ryker? Anything happen with him?"

I told Madeline everything, but this was a secret I wanted to keep to myself. If other people knew about it, it would make the arrangement more serious. And she would give me shit for going back on my word. "No. We had amazing sex, but that's over."

"I don't think I'd be able to walk away from that."

I couldn't either. When Ryker laid out the parameters of the relationship without a hint of emotion, I thought it could work. He didn't object to any of my requests, and even if he did, I probably would have caved because he was that good in the sack. The second time we slept together I thought it might be mediocre because the novelty had worn off. But nope, it was the exact opposite. "There are other fish in the sea, right?"

Madeline bowed her head and picked at her cupcake, not taking a bite but destroying the foundation of the baked treat. She avoided eye contact and suddenly seemed morose. The change was so sudden that it was jarring.

"Everything alright, girl?"

"Yeah..." She set down her fork and took a long drink of her coffee, slurping it down like something was stuck in her throat.

I knew she was full of shit. "Madeline, it's me. You can tell me anything." I set my fork down and watched her with concern, unsure what she wanted to say to me. She only acted like this when something bad happened.

"It's one of those situations where you don't know if you should tell the person... It might be helpful, or it might be hurtful...it could go either way. But if I don't tell you, you'll find out some other way, and that might be worse."

"Okay..." Now I really was worried. "Just lay it on me."

"Alright." She wiped her fingers with a napkin and released a big sigh, the weight of the situation suffocating her.

I waited, my eyes glued to her face.

She sighed again.

"Just be straight with me, Maddie. You know I can take anything."

"Okay, okay. Nathan and Lily just got divorced." The sympathy crept into her expression as she watched me, waiting for whatever reaction I might have.

I heard the words, and they sank into my skin slowly, eventually seeping into my bones. My heart continued to beat at a normal pace, unaffected by this information. But everything else fired up. My temperature increased, and my lungs worked a little harder to give me the air I needed. The news wasn't good or bad, but it was jarring all the same. "Do you know why?"

"No. Jenn heard this from Jasmine, who's friends with—"

"I know who Jasmine is." I knew all of Lily's friends.

"Looks like the divorce happened pretty quickly. It may have been mutual. I don't know…"

I tore off a piece of the cupcake and popped the piece into my mouth. I chewed it slowly, thinking of that horrific day when I walked into my apartment and saw the love of my life fucking my best friend. To this day, I wasn't sure which betrayal hurt me more.

"Are you happy…?"

"Not really," I said honestly. "It would have made me feel better if they were meant to be. Then I wouldn't take the betrayal so personally. But if they were only married less than two years...then what they had wasn't real. So Nathan left me because she had nicer tits and a perkier ass. No other reason. And that's what bothers me..."

Madeline nodded in understanding. "I get where you're coming from. But I wanted to tell you so no one else would catch you off guard."

"You did the right thing, Maddie."

"And just in case he tries talking to you again..."

I scoffed because the suggestion was ludicrous. "He'd have to be really stupid to try that."

"You never know. Men are thick."

"True." I ate more of my cupcake and inhaled my coffee like it was air.

Madeline watched every move I made, analyzing every little action. "You okay?"

"Yeah, I'm fine."

"Are you sure?"

"Absolutely." I forced a fake smile to reassure her there was nothing to worry about. But inside, it did bother me. When it came to Nathan, I would always be bitter. Not only did he break my heart, but he made a fool out of me to the entire world. Everyone I knew saw me as the poor girl that he traded in for something better. And Lily betrayed me even more. We'd been best friends since sixth grade. But all those years of friendship didn't mean as much to her as it did to me. "What do you want to do on Saturday? I was thinking we could go wine tasting in Connecticut along the coast. What do you say?"

"Sounds like a plan to me. I'll text Jenn." She pulled out her phone and sent the message. "I'm sure she'll be down. Anyone else you want to invite?"

"I guess Jared, unless he has a date. He told me he was talking to some girl from the gym. Not sure if anything came from it."

"It's Jared." She rolled her eyes. "Something always comes from it."

I laughed because she was right. Not only was he good-looking, but he had serious moves. He could land chicks quicker than we could land guys. He had a very special talent.

"What about Liam and Ryker?"

"What about them?" I didn't invite my brother to do everything, and I wasn't going to start now. I enjoy my brother's company, but we weren't attached at the hip.

"Should we invite them?"

"Do you want to invite them?" I asked. "Or more specifically, Liam?"

A smile crept into her features. "Yes, please. Unless that will be weird between you and Ryker."

"Not at all." I would just have to keep my hands to myself and not screw him in the bathroom while everyone was preoccupied. "Invite them."

"Alright. I'm gonna do it." She typed the message on her phone and set it on the table.

Instantly, Liam's named popped up on the screen.

"He said they'll be there." She smiled as she texted back. "And Jared said he'll come, but he's bringing a hot piece of ass—his words, not mine."

She didn't need to tell me that. I figured that out on my own.

"And Jenn is down too. Looks like the whole crew is coming. This will be fun."

"Yeah, I'm sure it will." I was grateful I had something to get my mind off what she just told me. After Nathan hurt me like that, I stood tall and refused to show my pain. I never cried in front of anyone or even let people think I may have been wounded by what happened. In fact, I acted like I didn't give a damn at all.

But in reality, what happened with Nathan and Lily destroyed me.

For good.

***

Stone Cold.

Ryker's message lit up on my screen. The nickname had grown on me since he first called me that. I liked it because it was unusual. I was sure he never called any other woman by that name. *Sexy.*

I miss you.

Am I talking to you or your cock?

Sweetheart, we're one and the same.

A shiver ran down my spine as I thought about the feel of his lips on my mouth. He was such a phenomenal kisser, the best I'd ever had. He used his hands with the same perfection as he did his mouth. Everything about him was perfect—the ideal man.

The more I thought about him, the more I burned for his touch. After the news Madeline gave me, I was eager to fall into something powerful so I would stop thinking about it. Sex with Ryker was the only thing good enough to mask all my other thoughts. I just thought about him and all the amazing things he did to me. *I want you to fuck me.* I didn't think twice about what I said. I didn't have any hesitance. With him, I felt like I could say anything without seeming desperate or clingy.

The feeling is mutual. Here or there?

I didn't want him at my apartment. When I stayed at his, I had the freedom to leave whenever I wanted and come home. But if he was at my place, I was at his mercy until he decided to leave. *I'll be there in ten minutes.*

We'll be waiting.

I left my apartment and arrived ten minutes later. I walked inside and finally noticed the qualities of his apartment. It was a penthouse on the top floor of a beautiful skyscraper. Hardwood floors led to floor-to-ceiling windows. His furniture was black and made of leather. Everything reeked of masculinity. "You have a nice place. I never noticed before."

He shut the door behind me then pressed his chest against my back. One arm folded over my chest and gripped my shoulder as he pressed his face into my neck. His lips brushed past my warm skin before he placed a wet kiss. My skin was so hot the moisture evaporated almost instantly. "Thank you."

He guided me to the back of the couch and pressed my hips against the top cushion. His muscled forearm was covered with corded veins, and his long fingers dug into my shoulder with possessiveness. "You can keep admiring it while I fuck you right here." He yanked my dress above my hips and pushed me down so I was bent over the couch.

I already wanted to come.

He pulled my thong down to my knees then dropped his sweatpants and boxers. He rolled on a condom then violently shoved himself inside me, giving me all of his length in one swift motion. He used to go easy on me, but now that my pussy was used to his cock, he didn't show me an ounce of gentleness.

Not that I wanted him to.

His hand wrapped around the front of my neck, and he slammed into me from behind, fucking me over the back of the couch. His cock pierced me over and over, sliding through the slickness that continued to grow just for him.

I loved the carnal aggression that seeped from every inch of his skin. He grunted from behind me as he worked his body to please me. Within minutes, he was covered in sweat and his fingers tightened around my throat.

I didn't prefer to be grabbed that way, but I liked it when he did it.

"This pussy is fucking perfect." He moaned between words as he fucked me into the back of the couch, taking me like he owned me.

He could own me all he wanted if he made me feel this good.

He leaned over me, his chest rubbing against my back. His lips moved to my ear as his breaths filled my canal.

I watched our figures move in the reflection of the black TV, two animals fucking in heat.

My hand cupped his neck as I listened to him breathe next to my ear, hearing all his desire for me in his pants. My fingers felt his strands of hair that were coated with sweat. I fell into the moment with him, forgetting about everything that happened before I walked through that front door.

"Come, sweetheart." He rammed his cock into me harder, pressing me into the couch. "You're getting so tight."

The fact that he knew when I was about to come just turned me on more. He could feel me intimately with his girth, feeling everything that my pussy felt from the connection between us. My channel tightened again, suffocating his cock with the reaction of my pleasure. Then I released a scream of joy, a shout of ecstasy.

"There you go."

I gripped the back of his head as I rode the waves of my high. He continued to give it to me good and hard, making the experience last longer than any other. The rush drained me, making me immensely satisfied. "Oh god…"

He kissed my hairline. "I'd love to be your god." He pumped into me a few more times before he released into the condom, filling the pouch with loads of his seed. He stayed buried inside me when he was finished, his cock slowly softening. "Fuck, that was good." He straightened and pulled out of me, making me feel empty once he was gone.

We both cleaned off in the bathroom before I pulled up my panties and straightened out my dress until it was no longer wrinkled. Something about screwing without even taking off my clothes was innately arousing. He couldn't have me quick enough, so he just did the bare minimum to get inside me.

Geez, he was hot.

He walked into the kitchen with just his sweatpants hanging on his lean hips. His chiseled physique gleamed under the low lighting of the kitchen, his mounds of muscle looking defined and sleek.

I could stare at him all day.

"How does shrimp linguini sound?" He pulled out everything he needed from the refrigerator and the cabinets before he began cooking.

"For what?"

"Dinner. You're hungry, right?" He stared me down with his gorgeous green eyes, a distinct shadow over his irises.

We agreed this was strictly about fucking, not dinners and romance. But we did agree to be friends on top of that. I didn't need to keep up my guard with Ryker all the time. He was clearly a player who never wanted a serious relationship. If there was anything I could count on, it was that. I was safe. "Yeah, sure. Can I help?"

"Get the pasta going, and I'll take care of the shrimp."

In perfect harmony, we worked together in the kitchen and prepared dinner like it wasn't our first rodeo. He had a big kitchen with lots of space, so we didn't need to fight each other to get things done. I paid a lot of money in rent for my place, but it was a fraction of the size of his penthouse.

"How was your day?" He worked the pan and cooked the shrimp, sizzling the seafood in the white wine and cheese.

I kept an eye on the boiling water, watching the linguini soften. "Good. I worked then got coffee with Madeline." I skipped over the conversation I had with her, not seeing the point in mentioning anything about Nathan to him. Ryker and I never talked about anything real. It was just sex and meaningless conversation.

"Liam mentioned something about wine tasting this Saturday?"

"Yeah, there's a few wineries along the coast of Connecticut. Should be fun. Madeline and Jenn are coming. Jared is bringing a date. So it should be a good time."

"Jared is bringing a date, huh?" He shifted the pan and made the shrimp fly into the air before they returned to the pan.

"Some woman he met at the gym."

"Good for him." His tone noticeably brightened. "Are we taking separate cars?"

"I guess we'll have to."

"Want to ride up with me?"

"Since I don't have a car, that would be nice."

He let the shrimp simmer in the pan, the sauce thickening into a glaze. "It's a two-seater, just so you know."

"Is it a fancy sports car?"

"Yep. A Vanquish."

"An Aston Martin?" I wouldn't call myself a car aficionado, but I did have a serious appreciation for luxury vehicles that I'll never be able to afford. "Wow. Those are such beautiful cars. And you hardly ever see them."

He turned off the burner while wearing a charming smile. "A chick who's into cars...that's hot." His arm circled my waist, and he leaned in and kissed me on the lips. It was a quick kiss, the kind couples might share.

But I liked it so I kissed him back.

He drained the pasta in the strainer then mixed it together with the shrimp he'd just prepared. "I'd love to take you for a ride then fuck you in the passenger seat." He made the two plates and set them on the dining table.

"You have no idea how much I would love that." I took the glass of wine he poured for me and took a sip. "But that car is too nice, you know? You don't want it to reek of sex."

"But then I would think about you every time I was in it." He gave me a smoldering look before he took a bite of his dinner. "So that works for me. But if you're trying to protect my car, you could always give me a nice blow job instead." He winked.

"Look how that worked out..."

"Or I could give you head. That works for me."

The idea of him going down on me brought me back to life. I thought I was satisfied and hungry, but now I realized I wanted another round. I'd never been addicted to sex like this. Most of the dates I went on led to nothing. And the ones that did lead to sex weren't groundbreaking. The scarce times I did have good sex, I wasn't this obsessed with getting more of it. Ryker was a rare breed, a gift to women from the universe. "How was your day?"

"Good. I went to the gym then played *Call of Duty*."

I didn't know anyone this young who was retired. Seemed kinda boring. "I don't mean this in an offensive way, but do you get bored staying home all day?"

He shrugged before he took another bite. "Sometimes. I'll probably get a job eventually, but for now, I'm just trying to relax. I'm kinda going through a hard time, so I'm not ready to do anything else at the moment."

We never talked about anything too personal, so I didn't know what he was talking about. "I'm sorry to hear that." I didn't ask him what suffering he was referring to because it was none of my business. I wouldn't want him to ask me the same question in return, so I gave him that respect.

He sipped his wine as he watched me across the table. "My father passed away about a year ago. Cancer." He went back to eating like he hadn't just said the most heartbreaking thing I'd ever heard.

"Ryker…I'm so sorry." The heartbreak thudded in my chest, his pain somehow transferring into my body like I'd lost someone too. Losing a family member was never easy, especially to a merciless murderer like cancer.

"It's okay." He looked up from his plate and gave me a look of encouragement. "It's something that will get easier in time."

"Is that why you moved here? To start over?"

He took a bite and slowly chewed his food like he pondered his answer long before he gave it. "Exactly."

I understood the need to start over better than anyone. To live in a place where everyone knew everything about your past was suffocating. I could never grow into someone else when everyone knew my best friend screwed me over and my fiancé left me for someone else. I permanently carried an invisible scar that everyone could see. "I get that. I hope you find exactly what you're looking for."

"Me too." He sipped his wine then stared out the window of his living room. The couch I was just fucked on sat there, the cushion dented in from my weight. His chin was dark from the five o'clock shadow that came in. I wondered how he would look if he didn't shave, if he let his hair grow.

He'd probably look just as sexy. "The food is good. Thanks for dinner."

"Thanks for helping me with it."

"I boiled pasta—a monkey could do it."

The corner of his mouth rose in a smile. "I always thought you kinda looked like a monkey."

I smacked his forearm playfully across the table. "I'm not a beauty queen, but I'm much cuter than a monkey."

"That's debatable..."

"Didn't seem that way on the couch."

He dropped his smile as his eyes darkened. "Felt like animal sex to me."

He got that right. I finished my plate then rinsed it in the sink. He joined me a moment later, putting his plate beside mine. As we stood side by side at the counter, I felt the electricity that I'd become used to. My hair stood on end, and I pictured that naked body on top of mine. Whenever his cock wasn't inside me, I was grouchy. This man was made to fuck me, to make me feel good.

He turned off the water then crowded me into the counter, my back pressed against the cabinets as he smothered me with his presence. His hands rested on the counter on either side of me, blocking me in like a cornered animal.

My nipples immediately hardened when he drew near, feeling hot under the collar. I swallowed the lump in my throat because my mouth suddenly felt dry. I tried to control my breathing so he wouldn't understand just how much his proximity affected me. But then again, he'd made me come enough times to understand just how much power he had over me.

"I want to fuck your mouth." He eyed my lips, making the command without hesitation. If any guy tried to tell me what to do, I'd tell him off. But in this case, I loved his authority. I liked being told what to do, not having to think about what needed to happen next. "On your knees."

I'd never wanted to be on my knees more in my life. I didn't care about getting my own pleasure because I knew he wasn't the kind of guy to leave me hanging. I kept my eyes on him as I lowered myself to my knees on the hardwood floor. I didn't care that it wasn't comfortable. I just wanted his cock in my mouth.

He yanked his sweatpants and boxers off until his enormous cock popped out. He held it against my face, the head swollen and engorged with blood. He gripped his shaft and ran his thumb over the head of his cock, smearing the pre-come that drizzled. Then he held his thumb to my lip, silently commanding me to suck it.

I opened my mouth and closed it around his thumb, immediately tasting him once my tongue swiped across the skin. It was salty and masculine, the best-tasting man I'd ever had. I sucked his skin until my taste buds couldn't detect anything else. I pulled my mouth away from his thumb, ready for the real thing.

He dug one hand into my hair and grabbed the back of my neck. Then he pointed his long dick into my mouth, pressing his shaft against my tongue as he slid inside. His eyes watched my mouth as he inserted half of his length inside me, touching the back of my throat. "You have no fucking idea how sexy you look right now."

I gripped the edge of his sweats and pulled them down to his knees as I craned my neck to take his length little by little. I'd never sucked a cock this large before, so I took my time getting used to him. Having a woman gag wasn't sexy.

Ryker rocked his hips into me, rubbing his cock against my flattened tongue. His fingers tightened on the back of my neck as his rocks turned into thrusts. His eyes darkened in color and his jaw clenched.

Saliva dripped over my mouth and down my chin. It slid to my chin then dripped onto the floor. I took advantage of the moments when he pulled out to take a deep breath, to get air into my lungs before his enormous length returned to the deep part of my throat and blocked my access to air.

Tears burned in my eyes until they bubbled to drops and slid down my cheeks. I wasn't crying, but feeling the expansion of my throat fired off nerve endings. I took him into my mouth repeatedly and it hurt, but it felt so good at the same time.

Ryker brushed his thumb across my cheek, absorbing a tear from my skin.

My fingers dug into his muscled thighs as I took more of him, wanting to make him feel as good as he'd made me feel over the past week.

"Damn, you're a pro."

I looked up and made eye contact with him, my jaw practically unhinged to take all of him. There were several inches I couldn't fit, but that didn't stop me from trying.

He brushed away the other tear with his thumb. "As much as I enjoy this, I need to come. You gonna take that, sweetheart?"

I grabbed his balls and gently massaged them with my fingertips. I gave him a nod, telling him I wanted every drop.

"You're a vision right now." He grasped my hair in his hand and watched me take his cock harder, crumbling into an orgasmic mess that was a pleasure to watch. He closed his eyes as he hit his threshold, thickening inside my mouth right before release. "Fuck yeah…" His seed shot into the back of my throat, spraying with mounds of heavy come. When I thought it was over, it kept coming, landing on my tongue so I could taste his pleasure.

I swallowed everything I received, wanting to keep my airway clear so my gag reflex wouldn't be initiated. My determination to give him a great experience kept my body in control. After all the amazing things he did for me, I wanted to return the favor in kind.

Ryker pulled his cock out of my mouth, soaked in my saliva. It was slowly hardening, the blood returning to his body and his brain. "Up." He pulled his boxers and sweatpants back on and yanked me by the hair. "It's your turn."

Chapter Nine

Ryker

She hopped in the car and fastened her safety belt. "Wow..." Cars were honking behind me, so I pulled back onto the road and headed out of the city. "Me or the car?" I grinned like the arrogant son of a bitch that I was.

She moved her hand to my thigh and gave it a squeeze. "Both."

"Good answer, sweetheart." I grabbed her hand and pulled it to my mouth, giving her a kiss on the back of the hand. My eyes remained glued to the road as I returned her hand to my lap. I purposely placed her hand in a spot where she could feel my hard-on through my jeans. It only popped up when she got in the car.

She moved her fingers around the definition of my length. "Hello to you too." "He's very happy to see you." She gave great head last night. It was phenomenal, really. It definitely wasn't her first rodeo because taking in a cock that size was a challenge for any experienced woman.

"That's funny. My entire body is happy to see him."

After we'd slept together a few times, she relaxed around me, turning into the woman I first met. She was playful, witty, and funny. Her guard wasn't up anymore, assuming I was going to flip on her and ask her to be something serious.

Never met a woman like her before.

Every woman I slept with wanted to be serious—or at least be monogamous. Austen was so determined to remain detached that it was a breath of fresh air. I didn't have to be an asshole like I usually did because she understood completely.

She was perfect.

"What are you thinking about?" Her voice shattered my thoughts as she spoke over the radio.

I didn't even realize I drifted away. "That you're perfect."

She rolled her eyes. "You were not."

"I'm serious." I grabbed her thigh and gave it a squeeze. "You're beautiful, sexy, a fireball in bed, and you want what I want. I don't have to be an asshole and break your heart. It's perfect."

She finally took me seriously, a smile spreading over her lips. "Meant to be."

I turned my gaze back to the road and drove with one hand. "Your brother tells me you're a bit of a heartbreaker."

"He did?" Alarm seeped into her voice. "You talked to me about him?"

"In a way."

"Did you tell him about us?"

"Of course not," I said calmly. "You can calm down."

"Then what happened?"

I shrugged. "I told him you were cute, and he asked if I had a thing for you."

She hung on to every word, leaning forward.

"I said no, and then he warned me you were a bit of a heartbreaker. He's never seen you with the same guy twice. He told me I should stay away from you if I didn't want to get my heart trampled on." I watched her in my peripheral vision, seeing her stoic expression. "Didn't seem to care if I wanted to date you or not. Pretty chill."

"And that was it?"

I nodded. "Yep."

She leaned back into the leather chair and relaxed, my hand still on her thigh.

"So, you're a bit of a heartbreaker, huh?" I kept my voice playful so she would know I wasn't interrogating her. "I better be careful."

"My brother doesn't know what he's talking about. Don't listen to him."

"So, you're saying he's incorrect?" Because it seemed like he was right on the money.

"He knows I don't do relationships and I'm never going to again."

Again. So she must have been in one before. Maybe it ended in a nasty breakup, maybe even a divorce. "Any particular reason why?"

She pulled her gaze from the window and looked at me, her blue eyes hypnotic with their beauty. "Why don't you do relationships?"

"I never said I didn't."

"So that's incorrect?"

I smiled because she had me. "Okay...you're right. I don't do relationships."

"And why not?"

I didn't want to answer her question, and she clearly didn't want to answer mine. We both had pasts that needed to stay in the past. "I guess we'll make a truce. That topic is off-limits."

"Works for me." She turned back to the window, clearly relaxed that we were steering away from an uncomfortable conversation. "I just wish people didn't think I was a freak for living my life this way. I know people judge me for it. It's okay for a man to play the field, but when a woman does it, she's a whore."

I ran my fingers over the bare skin of her thigh. "I don't think that at all."

"Really?" Her hand moved over mine on her thigh, her fingers warm from sitting in the sun.

"Of course not. I'm a big feminist. In fact, I think men everywhere wish women were more like you. Sex doesn't have to be a big deal. It could be an enjoyable event that doesn't necessarily need to mean anything. It's just an experience."

"That's nice to hear, for a change."

"So you never want to get married?"

"Hell no. Do you?"

I shook my head. "What about having kids?"

"I think I'll adopt a few when I'm older."

I wasn't expecting her to say that. "That's cool."

"I don't think you need two parents to raise kids that need homes. I can handle it on my own."

"I agree."

"What about you?" she asked.

I shook my head. "I have no interest in having children." The only time I did was when I realized just how madly in love I was with Rae. I pictured us getting married and having a family. It was the moment I realized I needed to get her back. "I have a brother, so he'll make my mother happy with grandchildren."

"Thank god for siblings, right?" she said with a chuckle. "That way the attention is not on you all the time."

"Amen."

I drove out of the city and finally reached the highway. We hugged the coast as we headed to Connecticut, enjoying the bright summer day and the sparkle of the ocean outside the window. Austen kept in touch with everyone via text so we would all arrive at the same time.

"What does Madeline think of Liam?" Was my friend wasting his time with a woman who was out of his league?

She set her phone in her lap. "You know this is a conflict of interest."

"Oh, come on. At least let me know if my friend is wasting his time. If he is, I'll drop hints here and there. I wouldn't throw you under the bus."

"Nope."

"You're a tough chick." Her loyalty was a turn-on. I liked a woman who wouldn't betray her friends. There weren't enough people like that in the world.

"You're sexy as hell, but that's not enough this time."

"Maybe I need to step up my game."

"I don't think you can."

I wanted to pull over in a secluded spot and take her roughly in the passenger seat, but there was no place private enough, and we needed to make good time. "We'll see when we get home."

"Oh…I like the sound of that."

I squeezed her hand on her thigh. "Going all day without fucking…that's gonna be rough."

"We might be able to sneak off behind a dumpster or something."

The dirty suggestion got me hard. "A public place…that's hot."

"Where's the most public place you've ever had sex?"

I'd had a lot of sex with a lot of women. To remember every single one was impossible. "The bathroom of a bar."

"Had to have her then and there?"

"She wanted to suck my cock. I'm a gentleman, so I didn't say no."

She chuckled. "You have an interesting definition of what a gentleman is."

"A man should please a woman—whether that's financially, sexually, or emotionally. And I think that blow job fell into that category."

"I guess I see your point. So if I call you in the middle of the night asking for good sex, you'll always be there?"

I ran my thumb over her small wrist. "I'm your boy toy, aren't I?"

"Ooh…you're my boy toy?"

"Yep. And you're my lady friend."

"Lady friend…nah. I want a better name."

"Like what?" I asked.

"Sexy friend."

"Alright. Sexy friend it is." I followed the GPS and pulled off to the side where the winery was located. Right off the coast with stunning views of the seaside, it was breathtaking. It was the perfect day for a woman to wear a summer dress with heels—which was exactly what Austen wore.

And she looked fine as hell.

Now that we'd arrived, I had to pull my hand away and cease all affection. We were just friends—not fuck buddies. It was only for a few hours, so I should be able to control myself.

But that was easier said than done.

***

Jared brought a cute date who mixed well with the rest of the group. She was attractive and funny, outspoken like the rest of the girls. But I noticed

Jared continued to look at Madeline, not being discreet about it either.

I wondered if his date noticed.

I suspected something happened between Madeline and Jared at some point in the past. He didn't seem like a guy who struggled to ask out women, so he'd probably already made his move. Maybe they used to see each other but things didn't work out.

Either way, I'd have to give Liam a heads-up.

Liam tended to Madeline, getting her a new glass of wine anytime her glass wasn't full enough. He gave her all his attention, laser focused. I could be making out with his sister right at the table, and he wouldn't even notice.

"Which one was your favorite?" Austen sat beside me, her legs crossed in the pink dress she wore. Her skin was tanned from wearing dresses outside so often. Her legs were toned and sleek, and I pictured the way they felt when they were wrapped around my waist.

It took a second for me to concentrate on what she said. "This one." I swirled the red wine before I took another drink.

"You're a fan of red?"

"I'm a fan of anything with alcohol, really."

"You're easy to please."

"No, you're just good at pleasing."

Her eyes widened in alarm at my quiet outburst, staring me down like I'd just told the entire table what we did behind closed doors.

I didn't give a damn because no one was listening to us anyway. I held her gaze as I drank my wine, wishing we were alone so her soft lips could wrap around my cock once more. This woman was good at everything in the bedroom. She was too good to be true. "What was yours?"

She went with the change in conversation. "I prefer white wines. I like the first one the most."

"Maybe we should get a few bottles to go."

"I drink too much as it is anyway."

We finished the tasting and the appetizers, sitting outside under the shade of an umbrella. The waves crashed against the shore, the sound soft like music. Sea gulls cried in the distance as they searched the beach for leftovers.

"I made reservations for Casanova," Madeline said. "We should head over so we aren't late."

After all the wine and the appetizers, I wasn't hungry. But if I got to sit across from Austen and look at her for the rest of the night, I would be happy. We left the table then walked back to the cars.

"I think I'm gonna ask her out." Liam walked beside me and kept his voice low. "I'm pretty sure she's into me."

That's when I noticed Jared watching us, probably trying to overhear our conversation.

I walked a little faster so we would put some distance between us. "I think there's something between Jared and Madeline."

"What are you talking about?" Liam asked. "He has a date."

"But he only seems to care about Madeline. I've seen him stare at her all day—and on other occasions."

"But if he was into her, wouldn't he have already asked her out by now?"

"Maybe he has. Maybe they used to date. Did you ever ask Madeline about it?"

"No...we aren't even dating. I can't ask her that."

"Maybe you could ask Austen." I could ask her myself, but I'd rather make it seem like we were as platonic as possible.

"I won't have any alone time with her today. Could you ask her in the car?"

"Yeah, sure."

Liam glanced at Jared, seeing him stare back at him. "Maybe you're right...looks like he wants to kill me." Liam trailed back to Madeline like he was trying to protect his property.

"Sweet ride, man." Jared admired my car with his arms crossed over his chest. "What year is she?"

"She's brand-new." I patted the hood like it was a pet. "She can hit 190."

"Damn," Jared said.

"And I get to ride in it." Austen posed on the hood of the car, looking like a supermodel trying to advertise it for a commercial. She flipped her hair over one shoulder and gave me a smoldering look.

My cock came to life in my jeans. "Now I want to buy another."

She laughed then hopped off the front.

"This is a car that doesn't need a hot chick on the front to sell," Jared teased. "But it doesn't hurt."

We got into our cars then drove thirty minutes to the restaurant, which was thirty minutes south.

"You wanna drive it on the ride home?" I asked.

"Are you joking?" she asked incredulously. "You would let me touch your baby?"

"It's not like it's a stick. You'll be fine."

"Are you serious?" she asked. "Because I'll drive this bad boy."

"Perfect. I'll feel you up on the ride home."

"God no," she said. "I'll definitely crash."

Now that we were alone together again, I returned my hand to her soft thigh. Her skin was warm to the touch, and I wanted to bury my face between her legs and taste her again. With the taste of wine on my lips and her natural sweetness, the taste would be orgasmic. "Did Madeline and Jared used to date?"

Austen quickly turned her head in my direction, her mood noticeably darker. "Why do you ask?"

"I see him stare at her a lot."

"Oh…"

I thought it was strange she didn't answer my question. "Is that a yes?"

"Uh…I…"

"Well, I already suspected it on my own, so you aren't betraying Madeline. And I told Liam my suspicion."

Once she was cornered, she dropped her hesitance. "Yeah…they used to be involved. It was a fuck buddy type situation. Madeline walked away when things became too complicated, but I don't think Jared wanted it to end."

"Why did she walk away?"

"Are you going to tell Liam everything I say?"

"Not if you don't want me to." We weren't in a relationship, but trust was important between two people who were screwing. It allowed us to be more adventurous, to take each other to new heights.

"You can tell him I confirmed that they used to see each other. But that's it."

"Alright."

"Madeline left because she was afraid of what it would do to their friendship. She didn't think it was gonna last, so she ended it before it became too serious. I think Jared wanted to take it further."

"Did he tell you this?"

"He tells me things sometimes because we're really close. But he knows I'm stuck in the middle so I'm not the best person to talk to about this sort of thing."

I couldn't help but wonder if something happened between Austen and Jared. It wasn't my place to ask, but I couldn't help myself. "Jared is your bestie, you said?" I specifically remembered her saying it because I assumed Jared must be gay. But obviously, he was just as straight as I was.

"Yeah, we're really good friends. We've been that way for a long time."

"Have you guys ever hooked up?"

She stared at me with wide eyes, surprised by the question. "That was bold of you to ask."

I really shouldn't care who was on her list of past lovers, but for some reason, I needed to know if Jared had ever had her. Something deep inside my chest rumbled with pure agitation. "I meant no offense."

She faced forward and kept her eyes on the road.

"So you aren't going to tell me?" I was pushing my luck and needed to keep myself in check, but the more she didn't answer, the more irritated I became. How did I know he didn't want to hook up with her again? That shouldn't matter either, but it mattered to me.

"I don't understand why you care."

"I'm not jealous, if that's what you're worried about." The second I said it, I knew it was a lie. I felt the despair in the pit of my stomach, a shadow of what I felt when I saw Rae with Zeke. It was small, nearly insignificant. But it was there.

"Then why are you so curious?"

"The more you don't answer the question, the more I think you have something to hide."

She turned to me with a fiery gaze, full of menace. But she just looked cuter when she was angry. "I thought we weren't going to interrogate each other."

"And I thought we were going to be friends? Don't friends talk? Tell each other stuff?"

When she realized I was right, she cooled off. "I'm sorry...I'm way too defensive sometimes."

"No kidding..."

She narrowed her eyes in offense.

I smiled then gripped her thigh so she knew I was kidding. "I like it when you get angry...you're sexy."

"I'm sexy when I'm pissed?" she asked incredulously.

"Yeah. I'm hoping you'll give me a good slap."

"I can't tell if you're kidding."

I gave her a smoldering look as I gripped her thigh. "Because I'm not."

She eyed me with slightly parted lips and bright eyes. When she licked her lips quickly, I knew she was thinking about the tension that just entered the car. It was searing hot like we were both being branded with a hot iron.

If there was somewhere to pull over for a quick fuck, I'd do it.

She reached across the center divider then unbuttoned my jeans and pulled my zipper down.

I took a deep breath because I knew what was coming next.

She yanked down the front so my cock popped out and rested against my stomach.

She leaned over and took my length into her mouth, taking it like a pro just like last time.

With one hand on the wheel, I used the other to shove up her dress and pull her panties to the side. I sucked my fingers before I shoved them inside her wet pussy, greeted by the moisture I was used to feeling. I fingered her as she sucked me off. We had another fifteen minutes until we arrived at the restaurant.

And it would be a great fifteen minutes.

Chapter Ten

Austen

I went to the gym after work then made dinner at home. I sat in front of the TV with my laptop on my lap. I was doing work from home, but my mind kept trailing to Ryker. We hadn't spoken since yesterday, and my body was eager for him like I was in the middle of an intense dry spell.

Which was preposterous.

Now I was getting unbelievable sex on a regular basis. I hadn't gone out to look for a date or even checked my Tinder account. The second Ryker was my fuck buddy, my interest in other men went to zero. I tried not to be alarmed by that because the situation was understandable.

Why would I look for another man when Ryker was already perfect?

I considered texting him and asking him to come over to give it to me good, but I felt a little self-conscious doing that. What if he was out with another woman and that message popped up on his phone? I would throw him under the bus with my horniness.

Maybe we should set up some kind of code or something.

I picked up my phone to call him, but my phone started to ring instead. My instinct told me it was Ryker calling me for the exact reason I was about to call him. But when I saw a completely different name on the screen, I nearly screamed.

Nathan.

Why the hell was he calling me?

Were my eyes playing tricks on me?

No, it really did say Nathan.

What did he want?

I watched the phone ring in my hands, frozen on the spot and unsure what to do. I didn't have to take his call. I didn't have to do anything. But seeing his number on my screen still felt like a breach of privacy.

I was surprised he even had my number.

I'd been off Facebook ever since that horrific day when my world came crumbling down. I didn't want to post fake bullshit and pretend I was okay. I didn't want people to scroll through my page and search for clues that showed how screwed up my life was now that I'd been humiliated. So I didn't have a clue where he got my number from.

Just before it went to voice mail, I picked up.

What the hell was I doing?

"I think you called the wrong number, Nathan." I kept my voice steady, full of unwavering confidence like a wall made of solid concrete. He needed to know his name on my screen didn't intimidate me. He needed to know that I could speak to him like he meant nothing to me—because he did mean nothing to me.

"Austen?" His deep voice was full of surprise, like he didn't expect me to pick up.

"Yes, sir. How can I help you?" My voice remained confident but playful. It didn't seem like he was ever my fiancé or ever anyone remotely important to me.

"Sorry, I was expecting your voice mail."

"Would you like me to hang up so you can call back?" I asked like a smartass.

"No," he said with an awkward chuckle. "I'm glad you answered...just caught me off guard."

"Well, what's up?"

He was quiet for so long it didn't seem like he would say anything. We hadn't had a real conversation since I found out he was sleeping with Lily. He didn't even defend himself or explain why it happened. It wasn't really a gruesome breakup because we just walked away from one another without looking back. So, that made this conversation even more awkward. "Can we get dinner tomorrow? I want to talk to you in person."

I laughed because his request was absolutely absurd. "Is that a joke?"

"I know you probably don't want to talk to me—"

"Probably? That's not the right word, Nathan."

"Look, I just want to apologize, Austen. Not over the phone—in person."

"You don't need to apologize, Nathan."

"Of course I do..."

"No, you don't because I haven't thought about you in two years. If you think I'm crying over you, I'm not. I'm a happy camper."

"Then why haven't you had a boyfriend since we broke up?"

My words froze in my throat because I was paralyzed. The fact that he knew my weakness, knew I'd been single for so long, was just humiliating. I didn't put up as good of a front as I hoped. "Because I love being single far too much."

I hung up before he could say another word and stared at the screen of my phone. I covered my face as the humiliation swept through me. He knew I hadn't been dating because people still talked about that horrific breakup. It was so embarrassing I actually wanted to cry.

"No, I'm not gonna do it." I shook my head and took a deep breath. I'd cried enough over this man, and I wasn't going to do it anymore. We'd been over for years, and he'd been married since. There was no reason to shed a single tear. It didn't matter why he called. It didn't matter what he wanted.

Nothing mattered.

I called Ryker instead and listened to the phone ring.

"Please answer...please be home...please be alone..."

He picked up after the second ring. "Hey, Stone Cold." The flirtatiousness of his tone washed over me like an ocean breeze. It was refreshing and comforting, wrapping around me like a warm blanket.

He did so much with just his voice. "Are you busy?"

"I'm never too busy for my fuck buddy." He always spoke with the sexiest voice, sounding like an in-demand phone sex operator. "You want me to go over there?"

"I'll be at your place in ten minutes." I didn't want to stay in this apartment. When I was at his place, I felt like I was in a different universe. Nothing could remind me of Nathan over there. He wouldn't be able to pierce an apartment that reeked of Ryker's dominion.

"You know, I'd like to see your place eventually."

"It's nothing fancy."

"But I'd like to steal a pair of panties from your drawer. You know, for another time."

That brought a smile to my face, and he didn't even know it. He would never understand how much I appreciated his perverted humor in that moment. I needed to be wanted. I needed a man to erase that conversation I just had with Nathan. "How about I bring a pair over?"

He was silent, but his intensity burned through the phone. "Sweetheart, you're the woman of my dreams."

***

I was in charge the second I walked into his apartment. I got him on the bed, his back against the headboard. He was already shirtless, so I didn't need to waste time stripping off a t-shirt. I pulled his sweatpants and boxers down to his thighs and rode him like he was my personal cowboy.

He gripped my thighs and watched me fuck him like my life depended on it. I rubbed my clit as I gripped his waist for balance. I bounced hard and took in his length over and over, working up a sweat and making my nipples as hard as the tips of knives. "Oh god…"

"If I'm a god, you're a goddess." He moved his hands underneath my thighs and helped me move with him, guiding me up and down his length when my legs became fatigued. His fingers dug into my ass, gripping the muscle as he held on.

I was about to come so I rubbed my clit harder, feeling the beginning of the euphoria wash over me. My pussy tightened around his massive cock, and I felt the explosion between my legs. A fire burned white-hot, and it consumed me from the inside out. I looked into his handsome face as I gushed all over his cock, my come sheathing the condom that separated us.

His large hands groped both of my tits, and he played with them as he thrust into me from below. I kept rocking with him so he could come as hard as I did, but my legs were so weak. He only needed a few more pumps before he ignited, filling the tip of the condom deep inside me. "Fuck…" He twisted my nipples gently as he finished, his eyes lidded with intense satisfaction.

I leaned against his chest and wrapped my arms around his neck. I gave him a kiss, feeling the sweat from our bodies mix together. Anytime his cock was inside me, I felt nothing but unbridled joy.

He lowered me to my back and moved on top of me, still kissing me as he went. He treasured my body with his lips, kissing me everywhere as he migrated down south. He kissed the area between my legs, his tongue exploring the most sensitive part of my body. While his touch was seductive, it was also relaxing. I writhed on the bed and enjoyed it, loving his face pressed against my entrance like that.

"How are you this good in bed…?" The words slipped out of my mouth automatically before I could stop them. When I was this high, my inhibitions were gone and I couldn't think straight.

He crawled up my body, the shine from my juice smeared across his lips. "Takes two to tango, sweetheart."

"But you're really good. I've never been with a man who can make me come like this."

He kissed my neck then the corner of my mouth. "You're high on the list for me too."

"Yeah, right," I said with a laugh. "You've probably had sex with all the girls on *Sports Illustrated.*"

"Actually, I've never had sex with a girl on the cover of *Sports Illustrated*. Oh, wait...I forgot about Britney."

I smacked his arm. "See?"

He chuckled then inserted one hand into my hair as he held himself on top of me. "Want to know a secret about sex?"

"Always."

"It doesn't matter how hot you are."

I looked him up and down, over six feet of chiseled muscle and perfect features. The first time I looked at him, I was wet. "I think it does."

"No, it's all about confidence. Just live in the moment and enjoy your partner. Be passionate. Be spontaneous. If the chemistry is there, the sex will always be good. I've had sex with gorgeous women who were just mediocre in bed."

"Really?"

"It's rare, but it happens. When I have really exceptional sex, it's not about looks. It's about more than that, like compatibility, respect, trust, stuff like that." He pulled my leg over his hip as we snuggled together on the top of his sheets. "And you are one of the best lays I've ever had."

"Even better than Britney?" I teased.

"Much better, actually."

"Ooh...go me."

He chuckled against my mouth and kissed me again. "I'll throw dinner in the oven, and we can hop in the shower. How does that sound?"

I didn't want to go home, so that sounded perfect. "You're going to cook for me again?"

"I can do more than just fuck, believe it or not."

"Then I'll take you up on that offer."

***

We had dinner at the dining table. Ryker was shirtless, thankfully. I never wanted to eat a meal while that man was fully clothed. Why would I deprive my eyes of that joy? "This is good. Thank you."

"No problem." He cut into his chicken and kept eating, using gentle table manners that defied his aggressive movements toward me. "You never told me what happened between you and Jared."

"That was because your dick was in my mouth."

Darkness settled in his eyes as he slowly chewed his food. "You can keep sticking my cock in your mouth, but you're going to have to answer the question eventually."

I finished my plate clean, feeling the dinner settle in my stomach. I didn't feel sexy after eating a meal, so I was glad we had the awesome sex beforehand. "Jared and I made out one time—that's it."

He pushed his empty plate away and stared me down. "Nothing else happened?"

"Nope."

"Why did you stop?"

"Because we were both drunk and knew we would regret it in the morning."

"Interesting. When I'm drunk, I don't have a single logical thought."

"It didn't feel right either." I remembered that night because I was devastated by what Nathan had done. I threw myself at my best friend so I could stop thinking about the crippling pain I was in. But in the end, it felt like I was kissing a cousin. "It was a stupid decision, and I'm glad it didn't go anywhere."

"Why did you kiss him to begin with?"

Dangerous territory. "I don't remember. It was a long time ago."

"Was it awkward afterward?"

Not at all. Jared knew I was a pathetic mess who had no control over what I was doing. I pretended to be strong for everyone else, that I didn't give a damn what Nathan did to me. But Jared was the only person I couldn't put up a front with. "No. Friendship lasts forever, right?"

He stared down at his plate, a distant look coming into his eyes. He seemed to be thinking about something else, something that had nothing to do with me. He felt his fork with his fingertips before he flicked it away on the plate.

I suspected Ryker had more problems than his father passing away. He seemed to carry a distinct sadness if he wasn't putting up a show for company. The darkness settled into his handsome features, making him look exhausted by an invisible burden.

I wanted to ask him about it, but I knew it wasn't my place. I hadn't told him about my demons, my own struggles, so why should he tell me his? We were both using each other to get off and forget about our problems—nothing else.

There was only one way to break the train of his thoughts. It was the same tactic I used on myself. I left my chair and approached his. He didn't look up at me, still thinking about past heartbreaks.

I straddled his hips and sat on his lap, my ass feeling his lack of arousal. My hands snaked around his arms, and I kissed the corner of his mouth and the scruff along his jaw, gently drawing him back to me.

Within seconds, he came back to me. His body hummed to life, and his hands snaked to my waist. He took control and kissed me on the mouth, his soft lips dominating mine. One hand moved into my hair next, touching the soft strands and gripping the back of my neck at the same time.

I loved it when he touched me like that.

His cock hardened in his sweatpants, pressing against my most sensitive area. His kiss became more intense as he fell further into the moment. He rocked his hips gently as he rubbed his hard dick against my throbbing clit.

I officially stopped thinking about Nathan.

And I knew he stopped thinking about whoever was on his mind.

***

His bed was so comfy. His mattress was luxurious, and his sheets were so soft. If this were in a showroom for a mattress store, they'd have to have security make sure no one crawled inside and took a nap.

He lay beside me with the sheets up to his waist. His bedside lamp was on, but that was the only light in the bedroom. He lay on his back and stared at the ceiling, one hand resting on his chiseled stomach.

Every time we had sex, it was awesome. I never walked away from a rendezvous without being completely satisfied. He either made me come because of his ego or because he genuinely cared about my pleasure.

But it didn't make a difference to me what his motives were.

We agreed not to do sleepovers, which was my idea, but now I didn't want to leave. His bed was comfy enough for a king, and I had a personal heater to keep me warm all night long. Plus, whenever I was with Ryker, I didn't think about anyone else. As long as I stayed in his apartment, I wouldn't think about that phone call I had with Nathan. I wouldn't analyze the conversation and try to figure out what he wanted. He claimed he just wanted to apologize, but I didn't believe that for a second.

So I closed my eyes and pulled the covers over my shoulder. I hoped Ryker was nice enough not to wake me up and kick me out. He agreed to my terms like they didn't matter to him, but they might be more important to him than he let on.

I hoped for the best.

Ryker didn't move from beside me. His body remained absolutely still. He could be asleep. With my eyes closed, it was hard to tell.

Then he turned to his nightstand and turned off the lamp, bringing his room into complete darkness. He moved his pillows and got comfortable in the bed, clearly preparing to go to sleep.

I was so grateful.

What would make this night even better would be his strong arms wrapped around me, his hard body spooning mine. If I were wrapped in his embrace, I truly wouldn't be alone. But that was pushing my luck.

Like he could read my mind, Ryker moved into my side and wrapped his arm around my waist. His head rested on the pillow beside me, his breathing slowly coming into my ear. It seemed like he wanted the same thing, not to be alone in this bed.

I wanted to wrap my arm over his and move closer into his side, but I had to pretend to be asleep. If I couldn't do that, then I would have to explain why I broke my own rule by staying over.

And since I didn't have an explanation, I didn't want to go there.

***

My alarm woke me up for work the following morning. It screeched in my ear from the floor where my purse ended up yesterday. I didn't want to get up, but I didn't want to keep listening to the most annoying sound in the world.

I kicked the covers back then lay on my stomach on the bed so I could reach down and snatch it. I turned it off so the bedroom would be quiet once more. Still half asleep, I rubbed the sleep from my eyes and fixed my tangled hair.

Ryker stirred from beside me, awake after the high-pitched piercing sound woke him up at the break of dawn. The bed shifted as he moved, and I could feel the dip in the mattress as he came closer to me.

He gripped my shoulder and turned me over, forcing me onto my back with my tits pointed to the ceiling. He parted my knees with his thighs then positioned himself on top of me, his hard cock rubbing against my clit as he moved.

A sleepy look was in his eyes, and his hair was tousled from my fingertips constantly running through it. His five o'clock shadow was darker and more pronounced, thick to the touch. He looked sexier than he ever had, fresh from a good night's sleep. "I want a quickie before work." His voice was deep and raspy, his throat clogged from not speaking for several hours. He pinned my knees back then slid his length inside me, pushing through my slickness that was always present when he was nearby.

It felt so good to feel him bare, to feel his warm and hot skin right against mine. It was a million times better than the latex that separated us when he wore a condom. It felt so good I almost didn't say anything.

"Fuck..." He closed his eyes as he savored the touch of our bodies. "Un-fucking-believable."

I wanted to keep going, but I knew I couldn't. I was on the pill, but this wasn't safe. "As much as I enjoy this, we need protection."

He growled against my mouth, a masculine protest.

"You know we need to."

"I'm clean, sweetheart. And I know you are too."

"And how do you know that?"

"Because you would tell me if you weren't." He pressed his mouth against mine as he continued to rock into me.

It felt so good that I didn't want to stop him. I wanted to feel his bare cock inside me, to sheath him with my wetness and take his come when he released inside me. The thought made me shiver with pleasure.

But I had to stay focused. "Ryker, no."

He growled against me again, but he stopped when I said the magic word. He pulled out of me, rolled on a condom, and when he was back on top of me, he fucked me hard like he was pissed off that he didn't get his way.

Which worked for me.

Chapter Eleven

Ryker

When my cock felt her bare pussy, I remembered how much I hated condoms.

Fucking hated them.

They diminished all the feelings, the sensation between a rock-hard cock and a drenched pussy. I wanted to feel her skin, to feel it clench directly around me as I fucked her. One of the first reasons I committed to Rae was because I didn't want to wear anything. And that opened the door to all the bullshit that followed.

I didn't want to go down that same road again.

But fuck, I wanted to forget the goddamn condoms.

Austen and I didn't mention the sleepover. She quickly got ready for work and left the apartment. Since I was awake and couldn't go back to sleep, I headed to the gym. I could have asked her to leave, and I would have had every right to do so, but I didn't care enough. And sleeping beside her was nice. I hadn't had someone stay over in so long I couldn't remember the last time it happened.

It was probably with Rae.

If it became a routine thing, I wouldn't mind. Austen's rhythmic breathing acted as a lullaby to me anyway.

After the gym, I showered and got ready for the day. My brother needed help with COLLECT, so I did some paperwork and sent everything electronically. He was still learning the ropes, so I did everything on my end and sent it over.

It wasn't like I had anything else to do.

At the end of the day, my phone rang.

Rae's name popped up on the screen.

I wasn't sure how I felt looking at her name. I had dodged her calls for a long time, but the conversation ended up being easy—like they usually were. But dread still filled my heart when she contacted me. I was at war with myself—wanting to talk to her and forget her at the same time.

I answered. "Hey, nerd." Playfulness was always the best approach to uncomfortable conversations.

"Trash boy."

"I don't work at COLLECT anymore, so I'm not a trash boy."

"You'll always be a trash boy to me."

I walked across my living room and looked out the window to the city beyond. The sun was beginning to go down as the day closed. I watched the lights from skyscrapers begin to shine as sunset approached. "What's new with you?"

"Safari got a brother."

"A brother, huh?" I hoped she meant she got another dog and wasn't announcing her pregnancy to me. That would be cold and something she would never do. "What kind of dog?"

"A lab."

"Oh, nice. Is he a puppy?"

"No. He's two years old. Found him running around the neighborhood, so we decided to adopt him."

"Just like how you found Safari." I still remembered the story. She told me one of the first nights I stayed at her apartment.

"Yep. Now Safari has someone to hang out with while I'm at work."

I noticed how she omitted Zeke altogether.

"What's new with you?"

"I help out my brother with COLLECT here and there."

"He's doing a good job. I like him."

"Not as much as me though, right?" I asked with a smile.

"Well, he's definitely not as hot as you are."

I laughed. "Good answer."

"Anything else?"

"I've been hanging out with friends, going out a lot."

"Good for you," she said. "I'm surprised you're still standing, then."

Austen popped into my mind, her brunette, reddish hair. She was playful and fun, and she was amazing in bed. When I was with her, I didn't think about Rae. Come to think of it, it was the only time I wasn't thinking about her.

"So…seeing anyone?" She couldn't mask the hope in her voice, wanting to hear that I found happiness the way she found joy with Zeke.

"Kinda."

"Kinda?"

"Well, I'm sleeping with this woman. It's not serious, and we agreed it never would be serious. But we've been spending a lot of time together."

"Why don't you guys want it to be serious?"

Did I really need to spell it out for her? "I'm not interested in a relationship. She's not either, but I'm not sure why. She doesn't want to talk about it."

"I hope your lack of interest is temporary..."

I rubbed the back of my neck as I stared out the window and to the city beyond. "I don't know, Rae... I just don't think it's for me. I had something great with you, and I messed it up. Maybe I'm just not meant to have forever with someone."

"That's absolutely untrue, Ryker."

Of course she would say that.

"We both know I would have taken you back if I hadn't...you know."

That didn't make this easier. "But we broke up because of my stupidity. I don't have the maturity for a deep commitment."

"Maybe you didn't then, but you do now. You're completely different, Ryker."

I wasn't so sure about that.

"Don't take it off the table, that's all I'm saying."

As long as I was still hung up on her, it would always be off the table. I'd been living in New York for nearly two months now, and my feelings hadn't changed. I found myself wondering what she was doing while I lay in bed alone. When I saw a game on TV, I wondered if she was watching the same one with the gang. Stupid thoughts like that popped in my head all the time. "We'll see how it goes..."

Rae didn't press the argument. "I just wanted to see how things are going. I'll send a picture of my new addition."

"What's his name?"

"Razor."

"Cool. I'd love to see it."

"Alright. I'll send it over in a minute."

I pressed my head against the glass and felt the coolness seep into my skin. I hung on the line with her, desperate to remain connected to her but also desperate to cut ties with her. How could we be on separate sides of the country but still feel this connection? Why did I have to be such an ass to her last year? "I'll talk to you later. Tell the gang I said hi."

"I will. Bye, Ryker."

I felt my throat grow dry before I spoke. "Bye, sweetheart."

***

I called Austen a few hours after she got off work.

"I love it when a sexy man calls me."

I smiled at her greeting, feeling the agony from earlier wash away almost immediately. "Not just any sexy man."

"The sexiest man."

I grinned wider. "Can I stop by?"

"Booty call time?"

"Something like that."

"I'll swing by in ten minutes."

I raised an eyebrow, noticing the subtle way she brushed me off. "Any reason you don't want me to come to your apartment?"

"It's not nearly as nice as yours."

"You think I care about that? I'll fuck you behind a dumpster, for god's sake."

She chuckled into the phone. "I believe you. But I don't like hanging out in my apartment."

"Why?" Why did she live there if she didn't like it?

"I don't know. I just prefer being over there."

That set alarms off in my head. "Please don't tell me you're married."

Now she laughed hard over the line. "Jesus Christ, no. Fine, come over and see my place. I've got nothing to hide."

I was intrigued by her brush-off, so I took her offer. "I'll be there in ten minutes. Send me the address."

"Just hit the button in the lobby, and I'll buzz you in."

I walked a few blocks to the east and found her building in a nice neighborhood. It had a doorman, so that told me it definitely wasn't a dump. The people going in and out were dressed nicely, like they were wealthy neighbors. The lobby was clean and music played overhead. I took the elevator to her floor and tried to figure out why she hated her own apartment so much. So far, it seemed pretty luxurious to me.

After I knocked on her door, she let me inside. The apartment was definitely one of quality, with hardwood floors, new appliances, art lights, and a large floor-to-ceiling window that overlooked the city. It was a fraction of the size of my apartment, but that was its only flaw.

"See?" She leaned against the counter and crossed her arms over her chest. "No husband."

"For now. Let's just hope he doesn't walk in while I'm screwing you in the bedroom." I moved into her and wrapped my hands around her waist. I had her pinned against the counter where she couldn't step away. I liked to corner her into things, make her my plaything. I leaned down and kissed her on the lips, feeling my mouth burn the moment we touched. We had intense chemistry, the kind that made my cock thicker than it'd ever been before. In the past month since I'd started screwing her on a regular basis, I hadn't been with anyone else. The thought never crossed my mind because I was so satisfied by this bed heathen.

"Maybe he could join us."

I smiled against her mouth. "I only do threesomes with dudes."

"Have you ever tried it?"

"No." My eyebrows furrowed. "Have you?"

She shrugged. "Never kiss and tell."

I couldn't tell if she was joking or not. The mystery surrounding this woman just made me more intrigued.

She ran her hands down my arms, feeling the muscles of my biceps and triceps. She touched my arms a lot, like they were one of her favorite features. "I missed you today."

"I missed you too." I repeated the words on instinct. I missed her anytime she wasn't naked and in my bed. I missed her whenever we were apart. Liam and John were good friends of mine, but Austen quickly became a member of my inner circle. I pulled out the paper from my back pocket and decided now was the best time to give it to her. "I stopped by the doctor's office today." I unfolded it and placed it on the counter beside her. "I'm clean."

She eyed it with raised eyebrows before she turned back to me.

"No condoms."

"We aren't monogamous."

"I haven't been with anyone." I eyed her and silently asked the question. A part of me didn't want to hear the answer. My stomach hardened in dread when I pictured another man thrusting inside her. I reminded myself I didn't care, that I was just concerned for my own health.

"That doesn't matter."

My eyebrow rose. "You've been with someone?" I immediately wanted to ask who it was so I could snap his neck and leave his body in a dumpster.

"No. But that could change."

Relief washed over me, but then the dread returned in full force. "The sex is amazing. Do you disagree?"

"Of course I don't disagree—"

"Then let's be exclusive fuck buddies. I don't want to wear a rubber anymore. It's fine for a few rounds, but after a while, that shit gets old."

Irritation immediately burned in her eyes at the direction of this conversation. "I told you from the very beginning that nothing would ever happen between us. This is purely physical and will never mean anything. I'm not looking for a boyfriend—"

"Shut up." I pressed harder into her, smashing her into the counter. "I'm not asking to be your boyfriend. I'm not asking for anything emotional. You keep being paranoid that I'm going to develop feelings for you. Trust me, I never will. You will always be just some woman that I screw—nothing more. You mean nothing to me—less than nothing."

Her eyes shifted back and forth as she stared me down, so close to my face that she couldn't get my entire face in a single view. Her expression remained exactly the same, but her eyes hardened in offense.

"You changed the rules when you slept over the other night. Now I want to change the rules because I want to go bareback. Safe sex is important to both of us, so I don't understand why we can't be monogamous until one of us gets bored with it or meets someone else. You're being a drama queen and making it into something bigger than it really is."

She crossed her arms over her chest, putting something in between us so we would remain separated.

"So what do you say?"

"Is this an ultimatum?" she asked.

"No. A friendly request."

"Then my answer is no."

I wanted to strangle her. "You seriously want to keep using condoms?"

"I don't want to be committed to anyone."

"We aren't committed to each other. If you find someone else you like, then we go back to condoms. That's it."

She shook her head. "No. That's my final answer." She migrated away from me and moved to the other side of the kitchen island, the counter between us.

I did my best to get what I wanted, but it backfired in my face. She was so set in her ways that she wasn't willing to entertain another way of life. Only someone who had been seriously screwed over would act that way. "What happened to you?"

"Excuse me?" she whispered.

"Something happened to you. A guy fucked with your head, didn't he?"

When her eyes slightly widened in fear, she revealed her answer. She did her best to hide it, but raw emotion was a powerful thing. She couldn't deny what happened. She couldn't go back in time and erase what transpired.

"A woman fucked me over too, Austen. But you know what? You've got to move on. I'm not some asshole who's going to pull you through the mud. I will always give it to you straight—even if you don't want to hear the truth."

Austen still wouldn't open up to me. She didn't ask me a single question about Rae because she didn't want a question in return about the man who broke her heart. She remained silent for minutes, just staring at me. After a while, she finally spoke, the confidence in full force. "I told you what I wanted from the beginning. I'm not going to change my mind. If that's not good enough for you, you know where the door is."

I snatched the paper off the counter and shoved it into my back pocket. I could go out and pick up a hot number from the bar, take her back to my place, and have wild sex. I could get a short-term monogamous partner until my desires were fulfilled. But I didn't want to do that. For the time being, Austen was the only woman I wanted. The sex was absolutely incredible, mind-blowing. Even with a rubber, she was still one of the best lays I'd ever had.

I walked around the kitchen island, my shoes thudding against the hard floor as I maneuvered to where she stood. I slowly approached her with my hands by my sides, my eyes locked on to her face. I walked up to her and looked down at her, sensing the chemical tension that rose between us. Despite her rejection, I still wanted this woman. I gripped her by the waist and set her on the counter so our faces were level. I yanked up her dress then pressed my mouth to hers, giving a kiss that expressed all my frustration. I kissed her hard with domination, claiming her even though she didn't want to be claimed.

The second her lips touched mine, she was on fire. Her hands went to my jeans and got them loose so my cock could pop out and greet her. She went for my shirt next, pulling it off my chest before she ran her hands over the slab of muscle.

I yanked a condom out of my pocket and pressed it into her hand. "Do the honors, sweetheart."

She ripped the foil then unrolled the latex onto my length, doing it quickly and efficiently. She cupped my balls at the end, massaging them in a sexy way as she sucked my bottom lip into her mouth.

She drove me crazy.

I pushed her onto her back on the counter then yanked her hips over the edge. With anger, I thrust myself inside her hard, pushing into her tight pussy and stretching her wide apart. The latex numbed the sensation, but it still felt so incredible that I forgot about our fight altogether.

I fucked her like I always did.

Chapter Twelve

Austen

I started to feel guilty for not telling Madeline and Jenn what was really going on with Ryker. I told them everything, just as they told me everything. And worst of all, I had no one to talk about my issues with because it was a secret.

And I'd never been good with secrets.

I knew they wouldn't tell Liam, so I didn't need to worry about that. And even if they did, it didn't seem like Liam cared all that much. It was none of his business anyway, so it shouldn't be a surprise. If he and Madeline hit it off, it's not like I would intervene.

I found them at the table in the back of the bar, sitting at their usual black booth in the corner. It could easily accommodate ten people, but we liked to hog it anyway. "What's up?"

"We got your cosmo, girl." Jenn pushed the pink glass toward me. "I tried to order two for you, but the waiter said I needed to pace myself."

I shook my head. "That guy doesn't know shit about pacing." I took a long drink just to defy the nameless waiter. "I'll straighten him out." "I'm sure you will," Madeline said. "So, what's new?

There's this new club that opened downtown. I thought we could check it out."

"Everything is new to me," I said. "So I'm down for anything." My parents were from New York, but I went away to college, and before that, I was in a private school in Connecticut. So I didn't spend a lot of time here in the city.

"Then we'll go on Saturday," Jenn said. "It's set in stone."

Now that I was with both of them, I felt the guilt grow in my gut. I'd been fooling around with Ryker for over a month now, and neither one of them knew anything about it. Madeline thought we slept together just one time, but that was only scratching the surface.

"You okay?" Madeline must have seen the disturbed look on my face because she flashed me an expression of concern.

"Uh...kinda." I cringed as I looked at both of them. "I need to tell you guys something."

"Uh-oh," Jenn said. "Please don't tell me you're knocked up."

"No." I'd be shocked if I were, since I was on two forms of birth control.

"Then what?" Madeline asked.

"So...you know how I said Ryker and I hooked up one time?" I stirred my drink and eyed the pink alcohol as it swirled around.

"Yeah..." Madeline narrowed her eyes.

"Actually, this is news to me," Jenn said. "How was he?"

"The best I've ever had." There was no doubt about that. I was madly in love with Nathan once upon a time, but Ryker smoked him in the bedroom. "One thing led to another, and it happened again...and now we're fuck buddies."

"Like, a booty call situation?" Madeline asked.

"Yep." I waited for the taunts and the criticism. I was going back on the promise I made to myself years ago.

"Honestly, I think it's great," Madeline said. "When you said you were never going to sleep with the same guy twice, I knew you were still heartbroken over Nathan. But if you want to keep seeing Ryker, I think that means you're in a good place."

That wasn't what I expected her to say. "But I'm not seeing Ryker. I'm just sleeping with him."

"It's still a start," Jenn said. "You guys must do other things besides screw the entire time."

There was dinner and conversation in between the sex. I even slept over there. "Well…yeah."

Madeline wore a yellow strapless dress that looked perfect on her, highlighting her skin tone perfectly. She was one of those girls who was naturally beautiful without wearing a drop of makeup. "I think this is a good start. Besides, he's sooo hot."

"It's never going to lead to anything. I told him that, and he agreed. But then yesterday he said he wanted to be monogamous so we could stop using condoms." I almost caved when he cornered me, but I managed to hold my ground. When he was silent and brooding, he was even sexier. I nearly gave in to him.

"What did you say?" Jenn asked.

"No, of course," I said. "That's not what I'm looking for. I told him I just wanted a fling—that's it."

"What's the big deal if it turns into something more?" Madeline asked.

"You know I'm never going down that road again." I didn't need to remind them of what I'd been through. "I'm happy with the way my life is. I'm not going to change it."

"For now." Jenn had her hair in spirals, gold hoops in her ears. She wore a skintight black dress, making all the guys glance in our direction. "What about when everyone else gets married and has kids?"

"And we're just going to stop being friends?" I asked incredulously. "We'll still hang out."

"But you won't have what we have," Madeline said. "You'll be missing out on a great experience."

"I'm sure I'll be fine, guys," I argued. "Lots of women don't get married and have kids."

Madeline and Jenn exchanged a look like I couldn't be more wrong.

"You know what?" Madeline said. "We've been really understanding up until this point. We know you went through a hard time because Nathan was an absolute jackass to you. You were hurt, and you needed time to lick your wounds. We totally get that. But, Austen, it's time you moved on."

"I have moved on." I was over what happened. I'd been with other men, and I was happy with my life.

"Not really," Jenn said. "You're absolutely terrified you're going to get hurt again. You're so scared, you aren't even willing to give anyone a chance."

"Not true. If I ever meet a guy I can't live without, I'll go for him." But I suspected that would never happen.

"But how will you know if you never give anyone a chance?" Madeline asked. "Why don't you start seeing Ryker seriously? He seems like a nice guy. He's successful, good-looking, polite, and honest."

I thought Nathan was the greatest guy in the world until he proved me wrong. "I know you guys mean well, but I simply don't agree. I'm gonna keep doing my thing because I'm happy. I just wanted you to know about Ryker because I felt guilty for hiding it from you. And don't mention it to Liam, by the way."

They both stared at me like they didn't buy my little speech.

I changed the subject before things became more uncomfortable. "So...Nathan called me the other day."

"Shut up." Jenn turned to me so fast she knocked over her drink, and it spilled onto the floor. "Shit." She grabbed a handful of napkins and threw them on top of the pool of alcohol.

"Who cares?" Madeline dropped more napkins on top, soaking up the mess and keeping it quarantined. "Austen, what happened? What did that slimy son of a bitch have to say?"

"Yeah?" Jenn leaned forward, her hands resting on the pile of soaked napkins. She was too engrossed in my news to care about the stickiness of her hands.

"I almost didn't answer." The adrenaline spiked in my blood just from talking about it. "He said he wanted to have dinner so he could apologize in person. I told him I was over our relationship so I didn't need an apology."

"Good," Madeline said. "Good response."

"And then he said he knew I hadn't had a boyfriend since we broke up..." I didn't know how he figured that out, but people talked. Everyone must have known I was sleeping around because my heart was broken so severely.

"Wow, what a dick." Jenn's eyes were about to pop out of her head. "What did you say?"

"I said I didn't have a boyfriend because I was too happy being single." In the moment, I couldn't think of anything better to say. I had to hold my ground so he wouldn't know how much he hurt me.

"That's good," Madeline said. "You don't need a man."

"He so did not call to apologize," Jenn said. "It's been almost three years. Three years too late."

"I think he's looking for a rebound," Madeline said. "Maybe he thinks you're still hung up on him so he has a chance."

"I never think about him." I definitely wasn't hung up on him. "So that's not gonna work."

"He has a lot of nerve to call you like that," Jenn said. "What a jackass."

"Why did they get divorced?" I shouldn't care, and I knew that. But now that he'd called me, I wanted to know.

"Not sure," Madeline said. "All I heard was they filed for divorce. Doesn't seem like anyone knows."

I probably would never find out. And whatever the answer was, it really didn't matter.

***

Ryker and I hadn't spoken since our fight slash angry fuck the day before. I knew he was pissed that he didn't get his way, but I wasn't going to cave—no matter what. I made the error of sleeping over when I shouldn't, but that was the last rule I would break. If I continued to make exceptions, I was afraid I would get myself stuck in a situation I couldn't handle.

At the end of the workday, I walked out of the building with my eyes glued to my phone. I wondered if Ryker had sent me a text message, but he hadn't. I suspected I would have to reach out to him since I pissed him off like that.

I was just about to type a message when I heard my name.

"Austen."

I looked up, recognizing the familiar deep voice. My eyes fell on the man I despised above all others. With a cleanly shaved face, striking blue eyes, and blond hair that I used to run my fingers through, stood Nathan—my ex-fiancé.

It took me a moment to absorb the reality of my situation. Nathan was really standing right in front of me, looking handsome in a t-shirt and jeans. His body was just as defined as before, beautiful and powerful. He had a natural boyish charm that just made him more charismatic.

Unlike on the phone, I couldn't find my ground. My confidence was nonexistent because my body was still in shock. Did he purposely wait outside the building in the hopes of seeing me? Or was this just a coincidence? "No, you have the wrong person." I quickly turned to the right and kept walking like I hadn't seen him at all. Sweat formed all over my body, and my heart ached like it would explode inside of my chest.

Fuck.

What should I do?

I wasn't naïve enough to think the conversation was over.

He would catch up to me in seconds.

It was only a matter of time.

"Austen." He jogged until he came to my side. "I'm sorry to catch you off guard like this. I didn't mean to scare you—"

"I'm not scared." I stopped in my tracks and stared him down. "You don't scare me, Nathan. You mean absolutely nothing to me. It's like you aren't even there." I started walking again, even though I was heading in the exact opposite direction of my apartment. Standing tall and proud, indifferent, was especially important in that moment. I would never forget our years together and what they meant to me—but I had to make him think I did.

"Austen...I know you're angry." He came to my side again. "I just—"

"I'm not angry, Nathan. I just don't want to be bothered by a stranger. I don't know you anymore. You don't know me. Let's leave it that way."

"I just want to talk to you, Austen."

"Go talk to your wife—ex-wife—whatever she is."

Nathan sighed, but he kept up with me, walking beside me as other pedestrians passed without paying any attention to us. "You heard about that, huh?"

"I would hope you're divorced because you shouldn't be trying to talk to your ex if you're still married. But wait…you're a cheater, and that's what cheaters do."

He bowed his head. "Okay…I deserved that."

"You deserve a lot more than that, Nathan."

"Can we go somewhere and have a conversation? I don't mind the exercise but—"

I stopped walking and turned to him again. "You said you wanted to apologize?"

His face lit up because he was finally getting what he wanted. "Yeah. So if we could just—"

"Apology accepted. I forgive you, Nathan. I think the best way to really show your remorse is by leaving me in peace. I wish you the best and hope nothing but good things happen for you." Okay, not really. "So, now that that's out of the way, let's just move on."

His face fell in disappointment. "Austen, I know you don't owe me anything, but I'd like to have a civil conversation with you. There are some things I need to tell you, and I think it's best if we sit down."

Those words meant nothing to me. "Nathan, when you left me for Lily, what did I do?"

His expression hardened into confusion. "Sorry?"

"When I walked in on you and Lily, you told me you wanted to be with her. Do you remember what I said?"

"Uh…"

Wow, he didn't even remember that. "I didn't fight for you, Nathan. I didn't scream at you. I didn't tell you how much you hurt me. I let you go, Nathan. I stepped aside because I knew you'd made up your mind. So I'm asking for the same respect. Just. Let. Me. Go." I walked away, and this time, he didn't follow me. He stayed on the sidewalk where I left him, thinking about what I just said.

I hoped that was the last time I would ever see him. Looking at his handsome face just brought back all the emotions I used to feel for him. He was the love of my life, the man I wanted to spend my life with. When he left, I'd never been in such a dark place. It was like waking up in a dream then going to bed with a nightmare.

***

I took the elevator to Ryker's floor then stood outside his door. I was just going to barge in on him and demand hot sex, but I realized how rude that was. So I lingered down the hallway and called him.

He answered after a few rings. "Sweetheart." He greeted me with his sexy voice, seeming aloof and indifferent.

"Hey. Are you busy right now?"

"I'm never busy when you call."

I loved it when he flirted with me. He was so good at it. "Do you mind if I come over?" I needed to bury myself in his arms and let his scent mask Nathan's. I wanted him to wipe away the memory altogether.

"Never."

"Good…because I'm down the hallway."

Ryker took a few moments to respond. "Why didn't you just knock?"

"I wasn't sure if you had company or something…"

"Then why didn't you call before you came over?"

Because I wasn't thinking straight. As soon as I had my conversation with Nathan, I jumped in a cab and ended up at his building. "Wasn't thinking."

"I'm not seeing anyone else but you right now. But you already knew that, Austen. So let's not play games, okay?"

"I'm not playing games."

His front door opened, and he stepped out, the phone pressed to his ear. "You wouldn't be standing at the end of my hallway right now if you weren't." He hung up and shoved his phone inside his pocket.

I kept the phone against my ear even though the line went dead. I stared at him before I returned the phone to my pocket and walked to his front door. I stared at his cleanly shaved face and his beautiful green eyes. I wanted to tell him about my day, about what happened with Nathan, but I couldn't bring myself to do it.

"I can tell something is wrong." He kept his voice barely above a whisper as his hand cupped my cheek and slid into my hair. "It's written all over your face. But I know you aren't going to tell me anything, so I'm not going to ask." He leaned in and gave me a soft kiss on the lips. The embrace was warm and full of affection, sexual energy that seemed to form anytime we were in the same room together.

His other hand snaked to the back of my neck and gripped me tightly, possessing me like I was his to do with whatever he wished. He guided me into the apartment and kicked the door shut without breaking our kiss. Next thing I knew, my back was pressed against the door, his jeans were around his ankles, and a condom was sheathed over his length. He lifted me up and tied my legs around his waist before he shoved himself violently inside me.

Then he fucked me hard and fast against the door, making me come before I even entered his apartment. He did exactly what I wanted, giving me such intense pleasure that I forgot about that ambush outside my work building.

My arms hooked around his neck, and I breathed into his mouth as he fucked me. "Ryker…"

He kissed me hard on the mouth and drove his tongue into my mouth, hips still working frantically to fuck me hard against his front door. "Sweetheart, I love hearing you say my name."

***

He had a large, walk-in shower that had plenty of room for two people. All the walls were made of glass, and the floor was made of granite. It was the most luxurious shower I'd ever been in.

He massaged the shampoo into his hair, the suds dripping down his hard chin and even harder chest. There was nothing more erotic than watching him bathe, watching him clean himself like a model for a soap commercial. "What?"

"Huh?" I replied automatically, losing my train of thought.

"You've been staring at me for nearly two minutes now."

"Oh…sorry. It's like watching porn."

He chuckled then massaged his soap-soaked hands into my tits. "If it was, would you be touching yourself right now?"

"Duh." Ryker was the sexiest hunk I'd ever laid eyes on. He was so beautiful I had to force my thighs together to keep them under control. He could make a video and charge a hundred bucks per person to watch it, and every single woman in the world would do it.

He chuckled at my honesty. "I've beaten off to you a few times."

"Uh…you were watching me?"

"No. After we met."

"Ohh…" Goose bumps prickled my skin. Now I was scorching hot, wanting more sex even though I had plenty.

He was hard—like usual. "I'd fuck you, but I don't have a condom handy."

I eyed his cock and tried to remain responsible at the same time. But that was damn hard to do.

He rolled his eyes then rubbed a bar of soap into his skin. "Geez, you're stubborn."

"I'm not stubborn. I just stick to my rules."

"Well, maybe you shouldn't have rules. Maybe you should just do what you want instead of preparing for the worst-case scenario all the time. You only live once, right?"

I was used to my friends telling me the ugly truth, and I knew Ryker was the same way. He would speak his mind even if I didn't want to hear it. "You patronize me more than my own parents."

"I guess your parents didn't do a good enough job. Now it's up to me."

I massaged the conditioner into my hair then let it sit, absorbing the moisture so my hair would be smooth and soft. "Your only job is to fuck me. I thought I made that clear."

"Well, I actually like you, Stone Cold. Need to straighten you out."

"You actually like me?"

"Yep. That's a serious compliment because I don't usually like anyone."

"Now look who's stubborn..."

The corner of his mouth rose in a smile. "So, what happened today? Bad day at work?"

My eyes fell in sadness now that the topic had been breached. I tried to avoid thinking about Nathan, but now that he'd shown up, it was a lot more difficult to accomplish. My main source of distraction was now reminding me of the thing I didn't want to talk about.

Ryker gave me a fierce look of disappointment. "Forget I asked. I'll fuck you when we're out of the shower, and you can head go home and go back to your life."

The insult ripped right through me, making me feel his rejection and my own pain at the exact same time. "I'm sorry. You're right. I need to loosen up a bit. It's just difficult for me. I don't sleep with the same guy more than once because then it doesn't work as well."

"What doesn't work as well?"

"The distraction. It helps keep me from thinking about things I don't want to think about. With you, the sex is so great I keep coming back. Anytime I'm with you, I don't think about my fears. So that's why I like being with you so much. It works..."

He rinsed the soap off his body and watched me with soft eyes. His anger and aggression faded away the moment I let some of my walls come down. "What are you so afraid of, sweetheart?"

I couldn't believe I was actually going to tell him this. Over the course of the last six weeks, I'd become close to him. I tried to avoid it as much as possible, but it happened anyway. I was tired of fighting our chemistry, the natural connection I felt since the first day I'd looked at him. Whether it was just physical or friendly, something was there. "It's hard for me to talk about... I guess I'm still embarrassed. I shouldn't be embarrassed because it wasn't my fault and I didn't have a clue what was going on, but it's still humiliating."

He didn't press me to continue the story. He watched me with gentle eyes as he waited for me to keep going.

"I was engaged."

The water pelted against his chest and streamed down his body, tiny riverbeds as the drops maneuvered to the floor.

I stepped farther under the water, welcoming the warmth. "I was in love. I was happy. And then I came home one day and caught him fucking my best friend..."

He closed his eyes as his jaw clenched, feeling the sting of the words once they'd been spoken.

"To this day, I still don't know how long their relationship had been going on. I don't know when they were hooking up or how it started. Lily and I haven't spoken since I found her on my bed with her ass in the air. And Nathan and I...we never really talked about it either. He packed his things and said he wanted to be with her. He didn't apologize...he didn't fight for me. He just...left." I felt the tears form inside my eyes. They were pressed down deep inside me, but I refused to let them emerge. Nathan and Lily didn't deserve my tears. "I guess I've never really gotten over it. I really did love Nathan. I wanted to spend my life with him and have kids with him. I'd just bought my wedding dress a few weeks before that..."

Ryker watched me with eyes heavy with remorse even though he'd done nothing wrong. His hands snaked around my waist, and he held me to his chest, the water crashing down on both of us. His hand moved down my back and along my side, soothing me in the only way he could.

I rested my cheek against his chest, grateful I didn't have to feel his pitiful stare any longer. Ryker was rough around the edges, calloused from old wounds, and I didn't expect him to be so gentle with me like this. It wasn't just about rough sex. He was more than just a playboy. "I found out that Nathan and Lily got a divorce. I couldn't believe it. If they were both going to betray me, I just assumed it would only be because they were destined to be together. But they barely lasted two years...really pathetic. So he called me last week...totally out of the blue."

"What did he say?"

"That he wanted to get dinner and apologize."

"Don't give him the time of day." His coldness counteracted the warmth of the water, chilling me to the bone.

"I didn't. But then, when I left work today, he was waiting for me. He asked me to dinner again because he wanted to talk. But I kept walking...and that's how I ended up here." I pulled away from his chest and looked up into his face, seeing the beautiful eyes that drove me wild.

"That guy has a lot of nerve."

"I know." After what he did to me, you'd think he would just leave me alone.

"You want me to take care of it?"

I chuckled because the question reminded me of eighth grade. "What? Are you going to beat him up?"

"No," he said quietly. "I'll fucking kill him." The look in his eyes suggested he wasn't kidding, but I hoped he was. "No…he's not worth it."

"I disagree."

I pressed my face against his chest again and kissed him right over the sternum. I tasted the water from the shower as well as his skin. "I haven't dated a guy since Nathan left me. It's just easier to have flings. A lot more fun that way. So when I met you, I made these rules so…nothing would happen."

His hands moved to my shoulders, and he gripped me gently. "So I don't want something more?"

"No…so I don't want something more." By sleeping with a guy only once, there was no possibility of getting attached. But Ryker was so amazing in the sack, I didn't want to give that up. I'd been doing a great job of keeping my feelings under control. But if we stopped seeing other people, forgot about protection, and had sleepovers all the time, I feared it was inevitable.

He massaged my shoulders gently before his hands slid down to my elbows. He maneuvered my arms around his waist, bringing me into him again. "I've got my own baggage too."

"You don't have to tell me if you don't want to. You don't owe me anything..." I didn't tell him my story just to get an answer out of him. I only did it because I couldn't keep it in any longer.

"I know. I want to."

I looked into his eyes as I waited for the story.

"I'd sworn off relationships my entire life. I've never been the monogamous kind of man. My father cheated on my mom a lot, and I saw his same flaws within myself. Then I met this woman named Rae..." He paused when he spoke her name out loud, like it was the first time he'd told someone about her. "We fooled around and had a good time. But I got to the point where I felt something for her, felt something strong enough that I didn't want to be with anyone else. I went into the relationship utterly terrified and not having a clue what I was doing. But she was patient with me, and we made it work. But then my dad got sick...and he and I fought a lot. I didn't know how to cope with it, and I never told Rae about any of it. Then she told me she loved me...and I freaked out. I dumped her."

I wasn't sure who I felt worse for—him or her.

"I spent the next three months sleeping with women whose names I never remembered. My father's cancer only got worse, and he didn't have much longer to live. But I couldn't forgive him for the things he did. And then he died...and that's when I felt everything. I couldn't avoid it any longer, and I collapsed."

Tears burned in my eyes, feeling his exact pain thudding inside his chest.

"I finally grieved and felt overwhelmed. But the agony forced me to wake up from the coma I'd induced myself in. I knew I loved her, loved her long before she loved me, and I worked my ass off to get her back...but she had already been seeing someone for a while. And she fell in love with him. In the end, I was too late."

I ran my hands up and down his chest, supplying a small amount of comfort.

"I couldn't stay in Seattle. Everything reminded me of her. So I moved here...to start over." He held my gaze, the pain bright in his eyes. "My story is nothing like yours. My misery is completely my fault. But I do understand what it's like to need a distraction, to need something just to take your mind off things. Ever since I met you, things have been a little easier. The sex is great, and just having a person beside me numbs the pain. But you never have to worry about something serious happening between us. The one time I tried to have a relationship with someone…I fucked it up just like I thought I would. I'm not cut out for this game. So if you're worried about us ever becoming anything meaningful, you don't need to worry about it. Because it's obvious we're both too fucked up to ever feel anything real for one another."

***

That conversation I had with Ryker was one of the most depressing ones I'd ever had. It was so raw, dark, and devastating. He was in love with a woman he couldn't have, and I was too messed up from seeing the love of my life run off with my best friend.

But it brought us closer together.

I didn't just see him as a sex machine with only one purpose. I didn't just see him as a beautiful man.

Now I saw him as one of my closest friends.

I didn't think about Nathan as much, but I kept thinking about Ryker. I wondered what Rae was like. Was she blond? Was she brunette? Did he still talk to her? Was she the love of his life the way Nathan was the love of mine?

I went to dinner with Madeline and Jenn after work, getting Italian food at one of our favorite places. We talked about mutual friends, Jared's new girlfriend, and the basketball game that was on last night. Eventually, Nathan came up.

"Have you heard from him?" Madeline asked.

"Yes...unfortunately." It happened nearly four days ago, but it still seemed like yesterday. I told them how he ambushed me outside of my office and followed me all the way up the street.

"Geez, what a psychopath," Jenn said. "Why is he so determined to talk to you?"

"I don't have a clue." There was nothing that important he could possibly say to me.

"Does he actually think you guys can just pick up where you left off?" Madeline asked. "He left without a backward glance. He never called to check on you. He never tried to do anything. And then he thinks he can have a conversation with you whenever he feels like it?"

"I have no idea what's going through that idiotic brain of his." But it was nothing logical.

"Well, I just found out that he's going to Vanessa's wedding next week," Madeline said. "I didn't even know he and Lily were on the invite list. But apparently, he's coming and she's not."

"How did you find that out?"

"Because Vanessa called me," Madeline said. "He's coming for Mark—since they were good friends in college. And she wanted me to give you a heads-up."

I dragged my hands down my face. "Ugh, I didn't even think of that..." I thought Lily and Nathan might be there, but I figured they wouldn't have the balls to show their faces if I was on the invite list.

"And since he's working so hard to talk to you, he's definitely coming," Jenn said. "It's just another opportunity to see you."

"Unless you aren't going to go?" Madeline asked, her eyebrow raised.

I wanted to cancel right on the spot. I didn't want to spend the evening dodging Nathan as he tried to corner me for a conversation I didn't want to have. But I didn't want to cancel either because if I did, he would know I did it just because of him. Losing face wasn't an option. "No. I'm not going to let him stop me from doing something. That means he won. I can't let that happen."

"That's true," Madeline said. "Then he would have power he shouldn't have."

"But do you really want to deal with him all night?" Jenn asked. "Wait, why don't you take Ryker with you?"

Making public appearances wasn't really our forte. We just shacked up together behind closed doors and had amazing sex. "Uh..."

"I did ask Liam to be my date for the wedding." Madeline cringed as she dropped this awkward piece of information on me, that she may be seriously dating my brother now. "So if you bring him, Liam will know about it."

My brother was the least of my problems right now. "Ryker made it sound like Liam wouldn't care if I started seeing Ryker."

"But then again, he thinks you aren't seriously seeing anyone," Madeline pointed out. "If he thinks this could be different, he might change his reaction."

That was true. But right now, I could deal with Liam's disapproval. I couldn't deal with Nathan nagging me all night long. "Actually, it's perfect. If I take Ryker with me, Nathan will assume I have a boyfriend. Then he'll back off for good."

"Do you think Ryker will go for it?" Jenn asked. "Since you guys are just...fuck buddies?"

Under the circumstance, I think he would. “Yeah, I told him about Nathan the other night. He would have to be a huge asshole to say no.”

“Good,” Jenn said. “But it looks like I’ll be the only one without a date. Ryker have any hot friends?”

“I could ask.” I’d never been introduced to any of his friends. But now that I was officially his friend, things could change. “I’ll see what he says.”

“Thanks,” Jenn said. “If he has a twin brother, that would be perfect.”

I laughed. “If he had a twin brother, I’d be taking advantage of that.”

“One Ryker isn’t good enough for you?” Madeline asked incredulously.

“Trust me,” I said. “I can never get enough Ryker.”

Chapter Thirteen

Ryker

Ever since that conversation in the shower, things had been different with Austen—in a good way. There was no trepidation, no secrets. I could be myself around her completely, and I sensed she felt the same way.

I offered to take her out to dinner since dinner was something we'd never done before. Normally, we screwed at my place, and I made something afterward. But now that the weight of expectations was completely gone, it felt like two friends having dinner together.

We went to a nice place on the Upper East Side, a restaurant I used to go to all the time when I particularly wanted to impress a woman. I didn't have that intention with Austen because she and I were in a good place. But that didn't mean I didn't enjoy taking out a beautiful woman for a nice evening.

We shared a bottle of wine, and I ordered the New York strip, and she had the pork chops. Candles were lit on all the tables, and couples spoke quietly from their secluded booths. A small glass vase contained a single red rose. It was definitely a romantic place.

She looked beautiful in a black dress with curled hair. Her lips were painted red, and she wore that dark eye makeup I liked. She was definitely the most beautiful woman in the world with those long legs and flawless skin.

And I got to take her home.

"This place is fancy pants," she said as she eyed the other tables. "I've always been a Taco Bell lady myself."

I chuckled. "Taco Bell is great—once in a while."

"This wine is awesome. How did you know?"

I used to date a woman who ran a vineyard. She knew a lot about wine, and when we weren't screwing, I learned a few things from her. "Someone introduced me to it. I'm glad you like it."

She devoured all the bread in the basket then moved on to her next glass of wine. Sometimes she made eyes at me across the table, the blue color beautiful and vibrant. She wanted to sink her claws into me.

I knew her well enough that I could tell.

"There's something I want to ask you..."

"To shack up in the bathroom?" I waggled my eyebrows.

She laughed like she thought I was joking. "This place is too fancy for that. In a bar, sure. In a Taco Bell, absolutely. But not something this swanky."

"Damn. I should have taken you to Taco Bell, then."

She laughed again, the sound spectacular on my ears. "As much as I love Taco Bell, I can tell this place is gonna be a million times better."

I watched her sip her wine again while I waited for her question. My legs were crossed at the ankle under the table while I held my hands in my lap. I hadn't worn slacks and a collared shirt since I left COLLECT, but now I was back in my old attire. I preferred jeans and a t-shirt. That was a big reason why I loathed getting another job. "What's your question, sweetheart?"

"Well..." She leaned forward over the table, her cleavage on display. I suspect she didn't realize it because she probably wouldn't lean so far forward if she did.

I kept my eyes on hers since this seemed important.

"I have this wedding to go to next Saturday. I was wondering if you would be my date."

That was it? "Sure. Can I fuck you in the bathroom there?"

"Absolutely," she said with a chuckle. "But there are some stipulations."

"Such as?"

"My brother is gonna be there. Not sure if that's weird for you."

Liam didn't seem to care if I dated his sister, so it shouldn't be a problem. We weren't really dating anyway, so it shouldn't matter. "It's not. What's the second one?"

"This is the bigger issue..."

"Okay." Now I was eager for her to spit it out.

"Nathan is going to be there."

The second she said his name, my vision turned red. Austen and I had only become close recently, but the idea of anyone hurting her like that was disgusting. He had the perfect woman, and he chose to trade her in for some faithless whore. I'd love to pop one right in his jaw. Fucking shithead.

"I would just not go but—"

"Don't not go because of him. Don't let him dictate your life." She'd better show up, her head held high.

"I agree. But I think it would be a lot easier if he thought I was seeing someone..."

Now her request became clear. "You want me to pretend to be your boyfriend?"

"Exactly," she said. "When he realizes I'm seeing someone, I think he'll move on and bug someone else."

"You don't think he'll assume it's an act?" He knew she'd been single for the past few years. He might figure out it was just a stunt.

"I doubt it. That doesn't sound like something I would do. And I wouldn't be asking you now if we weren't already sleeping together. It's not like it's completely false, you know?"

"I get what you're saying."

"So if you don't want to do—"

"I'd love to be your date, sweetheart. And I'll make him wonder what your face looks like when I'm fucking you. I'll make him wonder if I make you come harder than he ever did. I'll make him question ever leaving you for that classless cunt. Don't worry about it."

Her fingers moved through her hair as she took me in, the heat entering her gaze. She parted her lips slightly like she needed more air from what her body just experienced. She sipped her wine then licked her lips, the skin of her chest reddening slightly.

I knew what all those signs meant. "Want to take the food to go?"

"Oh, thank god."

***

I moved on top of her on the bed, my favorite position to take her in. She spread her legs to me, her fingers digging into my hips as she yanked me toward her, desperate for my enormous cock to stretch her wide apart. Her hair trailed around her face as it lay back on the pillow, looking soft and lustrous. Her lips were parted and wet from my kiss, her pants filling the space between us.

"I have a condition."

My statement brought her out of the moment. Her hands gripped my arms as she looked up at me. "Condition for what?"

"For being your date."

"What?" Her nipples were hard from the way I sucked each of them fiercely.

"I'll go as your date if we forget the condoms."

Her eyes narrowed at my request.

Now that she and I were at a new level of friendship, I didn't think my request was that unfair. "When one of us sleeps with someone else, then we'll go back to condoms. But for now, it doesn't make any sense. I want to come inside you."

Her cheeks reddened at the last sentence, her desire obvious by the look in her eyes.

"Sweetheart." I pressed my head to her entrance, feeling the wetness that pooled just for me. My head absorbed the moisture, feeling the stickiness of her lubrication. I wanted to shove myself violently inside her, to feel that tight little pussy bare once again. "Answer me." I wanted her direct audible consent before I went ahead and did what I wanted.

"Okay."

Hallelujah. I slipped my cock inside her, feeling absolutely no resistance like I did with a condom. I inched my way farther inside her, sinking deep as I moved as far as I could go. My entire body tensed as I felt the incredible pleasure rip through my nerves. She felt amazing, like the queen of all pussies.

She dug her nails into my arms as she breathed through the pleasure. Moans escaped her mouth, loud and incoherent. Her eyes glazed over like she couldn't even think. It was like the first time we'd ever had sex, and every movement was euphoric.

"You have no idea how good you feel." I slowly rocked into her, moving through the smoothness her body produced in arousal. My entire length was coated with her desire, moving in and out with pure slickness. I already wanted to come, but I was too much of a gentleman for that.

"Ryker..." She hooked her arms around my neck and kissed me, her hips moving underneath me to take my length over and over. Together, we moved our bodies to make each other feel as good as possible. "I'm already going to come."

Thank god. "Me too." I moved my tongue with hers as we breathed together, our bodies making sex sounds as they combined together over and over. My hips thrust into her harder because they were out of my control. I couldn't stop myself from rocking the bed, falling into her incredible pussy with everything I had.

I was desperate to finish but even more desperate to make sure she finished before I did. So I deepened the angle and rubbed my pelvic bone against her clitoris, giving her the extra stimulation she needed to come right then and there.

Thankfully, she did. "Ryker..." Her pussy clenched around me, her come gushing all over my cock.

I couldn't last another second, not when I could feel her bare pussy gripping my cock like that. I pumped into her hair, making my headboard slam against the wall, and I came deep inside her with a loud grunt. "Fuck." My cock twitched as I released my come, filling her with every drop I had.

She grabbed my ass and pulled me farther into her, sheathing my entire length as she took all my come. "I can feel it...so heavy."

I automatically grabbed her neck in response, suddenly feeling a new rush of arousal even though I was already satisfied. I didn't pull my cock out because I wanted to stay buried inside her forever, feeling our come mixed together with carnal satisfaction. "You're aren't going home tonight."

"I'm not?" she whispered.

"No." I kissed her as I felt my cock harden again, going back to full mast like I didn't just dump everything I had inside of her. "Because I'm going to be coming inside you until morning."

Chapter Fourteen

Austen

I bought a pale yellow dress for the wedding, something bright and summery that wasn't bright enough to steal focus from the bride. The straps covered my shoulders, and it was tight on my waist until it reached slightly above my knee. I did my hair in wavy curls and wore more makeup than I usually did. I shouldn't care about making Nathan jealous.

But I did.

Ryker picked me up right on time. He looked me up and down with approval before he gave me a thumbs-up. "Day-yum."

I chuckled and felt my cheeks redden, flattered by the flirtatious compliment. "You look nice too."

"Well, obviously. I mean, look at me." He spun around with his arms up, showing his tight ass in his slacks. When he turned back around, he wore a smile that told me he was joking. He wore a white collared shirt with a blue tie, the shirt fitting his lean and toned body perfectly. He didn't just look nice. He looked like a million bucks.

He moved his arms around my waist and pulled me in for a soft kiss, the kind that lacked tongue. He kissed me gently and tightened his hands on my waist, showing the passion as it began to escalate. When his tongue entered my mouth, I knew what would happen next.

"We can't do that." I pulled away before we fucked on the hardwood floor of my apartment. "We probably won't even go to the wedding if we start that up."

"Not the worst idea in the world." His hands gripped my ass playfully before he let go. "Ready?"

"Yeah." I grabbed the pink clutch I bought just for the occasion, and we walked out and headed to his car.

We drove out of the city and headed to the countryside of Connecticut. It was just a short drive away through the greenery that existed outside the skyscrapers of Manhattan. The wedding was supposed to be at a vineyard someplace along the coast.

Ryker rested his hand on my thigh as we drove in comfortable silence. His long fingers were masculine in shape, his knuckles rugged and carved out of marble. His forearms were corded with veins on top of endless muscle. Even the least sexy parts of him were absolutely delicious.

"What are you thinking, Stone Cold?"

The unusual nickname had stuck since the first time we met, but now I embraced it. It was nice to be called by a name no one else ever called you. And he certainly never called another woman by that name. We had something that neither one of us would ever share with another person. It made it special. "That even your hands are sexy."

"My hands, huh?" He grinned as he kept his eyes on the road.

I ran my finger over the top of his hand. "Yeah. They're toned and covered in veins."

"And you think veins are sexy?"

"Yeah. I think everything about you is sexy."

He turned to me this time, wearing a smile. "Great answer, Stone Cold. And the feeling is mutual."

"Yeah? You even think my feet are sexy?"

"Hell yeah. You could jerk me off with them anytime."

I covered my mouth as I laughed, stunned by what he'd just said. "Oh my god, are you a foot guy?"

"Not particularly. But I'm a Stone Cold guy." He squeezed my hand and ran his thumb over my knuckles. "I'd fuck your feet any day."

"I can't tell if you're joking."

"You bet your ass I'm not." He turned back to the road and drove on the solitary highway. There were no other cars, so it seemed like we were on our own adventure. The radio played lightly over the speakers, and we fell into comfortable silence. "Nervous?"

"I'm not the one getting married."

"You know what I mean, sweetheart." He glanced at me before he turned his eyes back to the road.

"Honestly, yes."

"Don't be."

"I know I shouldn't be. But something about Nathan makes me feel stupid things. When I saw him outside my building, I was angry and upset…but I also couldn't help but notice how handsome he looked. I couldn't stop thinking about the way he proposed to me. After what he did to me, I shouldn't feel anything but hatred. But I just…can't help it." I looked out the side window so I wouldn't have to see Ryker's face. "I know that's pathetic. I know that's terrible. I know anyone would think less of me for being so weak. Even I think less of me. But it's the truth."

Ryker was quiet for so long it didn't seem like he was going to say anything at all. "I don't think less of you."

"It's okay if you do…"

"I really don't. When you really love someone, it's impossible to hate them."

I wondered if he was talking about his own feelings for Rae. "He asked you to marry him, and you said yes. You thought you were going to spend the rest of your lives together. It wasn't like he was just some boyfriend. I think your feelings are understandable. I've been living in New York for over two months now, and I'm still not over Rae. I'm not even close." He positioned one arm on the windowsill as his hand rested on the steering wheel. His other hand remained on my lap. "If you're pathetic, I'm pathetic too."

I felt a spasm of jealousy when he confessed his feelings. I shouldn't care because we weren't serious and we never would be serious. But somewhere deep down inside, I felt the pain. I wondered if he felt the same way when I confessed my feelings about Nathan. But with Ryker's personality, I could probably figure it out.

"She's with someone else, and they're going to get married. I shouldn't think about her anymore, but I do—every damn day." He shook his head in disappointment. "So don't ever feel like you're alone, Austen. We've all been there."

I turned back to him, wearing a forced smile. "Thanks."

***

We parked in the gravel then walked toward the vineyard where the ceremony was about to be held right in front of the aisles of grape leaves. White chairs were in rows facing the white gazebo that had been placed there for the ceremony. I immediately looked for my friends, searching for Nathan at the same time.

Ryker grabbed my hand and interlocked our fingers. He looked down at me as we walked, giving me a look of silent encouragement. "You look stunning and pulled together. Just remember that."

"Thanks..."

He released my hand and moved his arm around my waist. He pulled me into his side and pressed a kiss to my hairline, his cologne washing over me as he got that close. I closed my eyes and treasured the sensation, the feeling of this beautiful man's affection.

We arrived at the chairs and found Madeline in one of the back rows with Liam.

Liam took one look at us, eyeing our affection, and then turned to Ryker with a raised eyebrow.

I hugged Madeline and Jenn before I greeted Jared and his date, McKenzie.

Ryker spoke quietly with Liam. I didn't catch much of their conversation other than, "I'll explain later."

We took our seats and waited for the ceremony to start. Ryker placed his arm over my chair and wrapped his arm around my shoulder, making me feel like I was the only woman at the wedding he cared about.

I sat there and stared at the view of the vineyards in front of me, trying not to think about where Nathan might be. After a few seconds, I felt eyes drill into my skin. It was hot and burning, making me feel like I was the target for a sniper. Without checking, I knew exactly who was looking at me.

Nathan.

***

The wedding party went to different places around the vineyard to take their wedding photos while we sat at a large table and enjoyed the cocktails and appetizers. Ryker didn't shy away from giving me affection even though Liam was there. He seemed to be more committed to make this day easier for me than being a loyal friend to my brother.

Madeline and Jenn didn't bring up Nathan the entire time we were together, knowing it was something I didn't want to talk about it. Besides, we were all thinking about it anyway, so it really didn't matter.

Liam wasn't the protective older brother type, but I was surprised he kept his cool even though Nathan was there. I suspected and hoped he would throw a punch after what Nathan did to me, but that didn't seem likely.

"I'm going to use the restroom." I downed more of my wine before I rose from my chair.

"Would you like me to walk you?" Ryker asked.

"No, it's just right here. I'll be fine."

"Alright." He squeezed my hand before he let me go.

I walked to the building where they housed the indoor bathrooms. The Tuscan design fit perfectly with Italian culture, and the hot summer day mixed with humidity nearly made me feel like I was there. I rounded the corner just as a hand grabbed me on the arm.

I quickly turned around and twisted my arm exactly as I was taught in my self-defense course.

Instinct kicked in, and I threw his arm down just as I raised my knee to slam it into his groin.

"Whoa." Nathan stepped back and protected himself from getting his dick broken. "Sorry, I didn't mean to startle you like that."

"Then don't grab me, dumbass." I didn't apologize for the harsh way I just attacked him. I didn't appreciate being grabbed from behind like that. "Saying my name would have been just as effective."

"You're right. I'm sorry." He raised his hands in the air in apology and stepped back. "Lesson learned." He stared at me with apologetic blue eyes, seeming sincere. Nathan reacted on instinct. He didn't always think things through before he did something. It made him both spontaneous and stupid, traits I once loved and hated at the same time. He lowered his hands and continued to stare at me with remorse. "Nice ceremony, huh?"

"Yes. It was a lot nicer than ours would have been."

His eyes fell at the insult. "I deserved that one too…"

"Nathan, what is your deal?" I looked around to make sure we were alone. I would be embarrassed to be seen having this conversation with my former fiancé. "Why won't you just leave me alone?"

"Because I want to talk to you—as I've said many times."

I rolled my eyes. "Why don't you just leave a voice mail, and I'll listen to it when I'm bored?" I'd turned into a vicious woman, when I didn't think I had it in me. Most of those words popped into my head from nowhere.

"Just one meal," he begged. "Come on."

"Why are you talking to me like I owe you something?"

"You don't owe me anything," he said. "I just want thirty minutes of your time. Think about it, if you have a meal with me, I'll leave you alone. You'll get what you want."

"So you're blackmailing me?" I crossed my arms over my chest and glared at him. "You'll only leave me alone if I give you what you want?"

"No, not at all." He threw his arms down. "I didn't mean for it to come out like that. I'm sorry. I just… I'm desperate, Austen. I'll do anything for thirty minutes of your time."

"Why?" I didn't understand why he was so eager to talk to me. There was nothing important enough he could possibly tell me. There certainly wasn't anything he could say to justify what he did to me. "Why is this so important to you?"

"Because you're important to me, Austen. I need to set the record straight. I need to explain why I did what I did."

"But I don't care what your reasoning was, Nathan." Actually, I did. It was something that still kept me up in the middle of the night sometimes. But if I showed I still cared, he won this battle.

"What can I do to change your mind?"

"You could have been faithful to me and married me," I snapped. "Then I'd do whatever you wanted, Nathan. But you decided to fuck my best friend instead. Sorry that you aren't getting your way."

He didn't cringe this time. "You can keep insulting me because I deserve it. I'll never tell you to stop. But can we do it over dinner? Can we just sit down and talk about what happened all those years ago?"

I knew Nathan wasn't going to stop until he got what he wanted. And honestly, I was eager to have this conversation. I wanted closure. I wanted to really move on and start a new life. I wanted to have believe in love again, to find someone new and settle down. Until I put this behind me, I wouldn't be able to do that. "Fine."

His entire face lit up when I finally agreed. "Really?"

I nodded.

"Thank you so much, Austen. Really."

I kept my arms folded over my chest, my guard still up. "When and where?"

"How about breakfast tomorrow?"

I planned on sleeping in with Ryker. I definitely didn't want to sleep alone tonight. "Dinner tomorrow night."

"That works for me. Thank you again. I really appreciate it."

I glanced over his shoulder and saw Ryker heading this way. In the collared shirt and tie, he looked like a million bucks. He was strong and powerful, domineering and graceful. His eyes were trained on Nathan like he was going to rip his head off when he arrived. "My boyfriend is right behind you, so I suggest you run."

Disappointment entered his eyes. "Oh…I thought you weren't seeing anyone."

"We've kept our relationship low profile for a few months. But now things have really picked up."

Nathan didn't take off like I thought he would. He stood his ground.

Ryker walked past him, purposely giving him a slight shove with his strong shoulder. He moved into me, snaking his arms around my waist and kissing me hard on the mouth, claiming his territory for the entire world to see. He kissed me like he loved me, like I was the most beautiful woman underneath that summer sky.

He was such a great kisser I nearly forgot about Nathan standing right there.

Ryker pulled away and turned back to Nathan, giving him a terrifying look. "Can I help you with something?"

Nathan didn't back down, but he didn't provoke him either. "No. Austen and I just finished our conversation."

"Good. Now you can crawl back to where you came from, cockroach."

Fury flashed in Nathan's eyes, but he didn't give in to his temper. He gave a slight nod before he dismissed himself. He probably didn't put up a stronger fight because he got what he wanted out of me. There was no need to make things worse.

When he was out of earshot, Ryker turned back to me. "You alright?"

"Yeah, I'm fine."

"Looks like I can't let you out of my sight."

"I think he'll leave me alone now."

"Just to be safe, I'm sticking to you like glue for the rest of the evening."

I ran my hands down his chest and smiled. "That sounds good to me."

Chapter Fifteen

Ryker

I spun Austen around before I pulled her back into me, guiding her during the slow song. She and I moved together just the way we did during sex—perfectly in sync. She anticipated my moves before I made them, and she carried herself with exquisite grace like she rehearsed our dance before we even met.

I pressed my face close to hers, smelling the summer grass and her perfume. She was easy to guide, even in heels, and I'd never loved dancing as much as I did with her. The last dance I had was with Rae for a COLLECT fundraiser, and it lasted two minutes before Zeke showed up. "You dance well."

"You're the one calling the shots."

"But you do a great job obeying."

"I'm quite the plaything."

I chuckled before I kissed her on the mouth, not caring if anyone was watching us. "When is this thing over so we can—"

"Mind if I cut in?" Madeline appeared, in a royal blue dress with diamond earrings. She stole the attention of most of the men just the way Austen did.

I reluctantly let her go, knowing I'd been replaced. "Sure. But I want her back when you're finished."

Madeline took my place and danced with Austen, the girls giggling as they whispered to one another.

I smiled before I walked back to my chair where my glass of wine was waiting for me. Liam was there, talking quietly with Jared and his date. Once I returned, he immediately turned to me and asked the question that had been on his mind all night. "So you and Austen, huh?"

I glanced around the tables and searched for Nathan. He was on the other side of the pavilion talking with friends. His eyes were on Austen, not me. "It's mostly an act."

"An act?" he asked.

"You know, because of Nathan."

He finally nodded in understanding. "Gotcha."

"She was nervous about tonight and asked me to pretend to be her boyfriend. We're close friends, so I agreed."

"Okay, that makes a lot more sense now. Austen doesn't seem like your type."

Not my type? Was he crazy? "Why do you say that?"

"She's just so bossy and domineering, you know?"

Actually, I liked that—a lot.

"And like I said, her track record isn't so great."

"Maybe she just hasn't met the right guy." I didn't know what possessed me to say that. I certainly wasn't the right guy she was looking for. She pretty much confessed she still had feelings for her ex-fiancé, and I was still hung up on the only woman I'd ever loved.

"I don't think she ever will. She's pretty set in her ways. But do what you want. Just be good to her, alright?"

"Of course, man." I feared Liam would be a lot more upset about me spending time with his younger sister, but he didn't seem to care at all. He believed she could handle herself. It was refreshing compared to my experience with Rex—who was a nightmare. If I just looked at Rae's hand, he acted like it was the end of the world.

"She's been through a lot, and I just want her to be happy. She seems happy without having a man around. And if that works for her, great. I want it to stay that way." He eyed the girls dancing together on the dance floor, laughing and having a great time.

"I'm just not thrilled she stole my date for the evening."

"You know what I would do if I were you?"

"Hmm?"

"Steal her back."

***

I drove into the city while Austen slept in the passenger seat in the car. I didn't want to take her home because I was hoping for sex before bed. After spending the entire afternoon with her looking absolutely sexy, I wanted to fuck her until I was satisfied.

She stirred once the bright lights from the streets shone through the window. She sat up straight, her eyes lidded and heavy.

"Hey, sweetheart." I ran my hand through her hair, feeling the soft strands brush against my skin.

"Sorry, I didn't mean to fall asleep."

"That's okay. You want to come back to my place?" My question implied she would be sleeping over, and I hoped she would take the bait. We'd broken a lot of rules that we established, so what was one more?

"Sure."

"Good. I was driving back to my apartment regardless."

She chuckled. "Then why did you ask?"

"I like to give you the illusion you have a choice, even if you don't. Makes me seem like a gentleman."

"If you care that much, you could just be a gentleman."

After a quick consideration, I shook my head. "Nah. Not my style."

She chuckled then moved her hand to my thigh. The simple touch brought my cock to life. The affection was gentle, borderline juvenile. But when it came to this woman, that was all I needed.

I parked the car in the underground garage, and then we took the elevator to the top floor. Once we were inside, the clothes dropped into piles on the floor, and we got naked under the sheets. It was a relief to fool around and then shove myself inside her without pausing to get a condom on.

And she felt incredible.

I took her from behind, staring at that beautiful ass and that gorgeous asshole. She was so wet she was practically slippery. Now that I was used to the unbelievable feeling of her bare pussy, I could control myself and last longer. I got to really enjoy the sex, to savor the feeling of her skin against mine.

Then I made her come just as hard as I did the first time we were together. But instead of letting myself go, I turned her on her back and thrust into her even harder, wanting to make her sore the following day.

She gripped my ass and pulled me harder into her, panting with moans that did amazing things to my ego. She tightened again, coating my cock in her come. "I want you to come inside me…"

"Here it comes…" I smashed my headboard into the wall as I pounded into home plate. Like lightning burst through my veins, I was white-hot and burning. My body reached the heavens as the most exquisite feeling came over me. I was hot and I was cold. I was dead and I was alive. "Fuck." I released inside her, giving her every drop and filling her to the brim. Nothing made me feel more like a man than coming inside a woman.

She wrapped her legs around my waist and pulled me in for a final kiss. "That was amazing…"

"You make me amazing."

She kissed the sweat on my chest then ran her hands up my back, massaging the areas that she previous scratched.

I didn't want to pull out of my new home, but I was tired and I knew she was too. I slowly pulled my soft dick out then lay beside her. The bedroom was already dark because I never bothered to turn on the lights.

She immediately moved into my side and hooked her arm around my waist, her hair all over the place.

I was hot and sweaty, as I usually was after sex. I didn't want to cuddle with anyone, and I usually told them to stick to their side of the bed. But I didn't mind having Austen beside me. She was soft, and she smelled good. So I let the affection linger. "Good night, Stone Cold."

She didn't say anything back because she was already asleep.

***

When I woke up the following morning, she was tucked into my side and our arms were tangled together. Her hair was in my face, and my leg was hooked around hers. It seemed like we rolled around all night—but we always stayed together.

I woke up first and blinked my eyes to adjust to the morning light. She smelled the same as she did last night, but now a hint of sex was ingrained in her skin. I liked smelling myself on her.

She woke up next, stretching beside me until she opened her eyes. She looked at me, her blue eyes still lazy with sleep. After a few seconds of taking me in, she smiled. "Morning, sexy man."

"Morning, sexy lady."

She pulled the sheet over her shoulder again. "Jesus Christ, this bed is comfortable."

"Macy's."

"Can I rent it out?"

"Sure. I'll collect in the form of sex." I wrapped my arm around her waist and leaned in for a kiss.

"That's a fair price. Consider it done." She kissed me back, not caring that neither one of us had brushed our teeth.

"After some morning sex, you want to get brunch?"

"Brunch, huh?"

"Yeah. You know, breakfast and lunch. I'm surprised you've never heard of it."

She smacked my arm. "Yes, I've heard of it. I'm just surprised."

"Why?"

"Kinda girly."

"It's not girly when I'm sipping a mimosa while staring at a beautiful woman across from me."

"And after some good morning sex beforehand."

"Exactly." I moved on top of her and got down to business, bareback.

After we finished, we threw on our clothes and walked down the block to a breakfast place. She fixed her hair with just her fingers and didn't wear makeup. It was one of the rare times when I saw her with a fresh face, clean skin without dark colors around her eyes. I liked it a lot, actually. All she did was brush her teeth—with my toothbrush. With minimal effort, she looked amazing.

We got a table and ordered our mimosas. She ordered the French toast, and I ordered the waffles. We decided to split a plate of eggs, bacon, and toast since neither one of us had the appetite to get a whole meal ourselves.

I wore jeans and a black t-shirt, back to my normal attire. Wearing a tie, even for an afternoon, was aggravating. I didn't like it at all. If I could take it a step further and just wear my boxers everywhere I went, I would. I'd probably get arrested, though. "Have a good time last night?"

"Actually, yeah."

"I'm glad Nathan didn't ruin it for you."

"I would let him ruin anything for me—again." She drank half of her glass then licked her lips. "Alcohol first thing in the morning...I love Sundays."

I tapped my glass against hers before I drank mine. "What did he say to you?" I didn't ask her last night because there wasn't an opportunity. Too many people were around.

"That he wanted to talk...like last time."

"Committed, isn't he?"

She stared at her glass, her eyes falling and the sadness creeping into her features.

"What is it?"

"He asked me to have dinner with him tonight." She raised her eyes again and looked at me. "And I said yes."

Something painful unleashed in my chest, although I couldn't identify what it was. Was I angry because I was protective of her? She'd become one of the closest people to me, and I cared a lot about her. I didn't want her anywhere near someone who didn't deserve her. Or was it something else?

She read my expression and understood my feelings about it. "I know it's not the smartest idea—"

"Because it's the dumbest." I wouldn't sugarcoat anything with her. She always got the truth from me—no matter how cold it was.

"But he keeps pursuing me, and I need some closure anyway. I've been trying to convince myself for the past few years that I'm okay...but I'm obviously not. I think I may need this as much as he does."

"I don't agree with that."

Her eyes looked into mine, the usual strength absent. "You're mad at me..."

"Not mad."

"Upset?"

"No."

"Then what?"

"Disappointed," I said quietly. "You're too good for him, sweetheart."

"I'm not getting back together with him. I'm just having dinner with him. I'm just talking to him."

Maybe I was skipping ahead and making unfair assumptions. "I suppose that's true."

"I'm always going to want to know what happened between us. I'm always going to want to know why he left."

"I can make it very simple for you," I said coldly. "He didn't love you, Austen. When a man loves a woman, he doesn't even look at other women. Trust me on that." When Rae and I were together, I kept my hands and eyes to myself. My loyalty was undeniable. To run off with another woman, especially her best friend, was despicable.

My words obviously wounded her because she broke eye contact and looked out the window, the sadness obvious in her expression. Her fingers played with the stem of her glass, and she clearly didn't feel comfortable around me anymore.

I was such an asshole.

"That was out of line," I said quietly. "I'm sorry."

"Don't apologize," she said quickly. "Never be sorry for being honest."

"It was still insensitive to say. I know this is hard for you."

"Really, it's okay." She drank the mimosa then finally looked at me again. Now her look was more guarded, like I might say something to wound her again.

I still felt bad. "If you think it'll make you feel better, then you should go."

"Yeah?"

I didn't agree with that at all, but I was trying to be reasonable. "It's your decision, Austen. I'll respect whatever you decide." As a friend, I was supposed to be supportive. I shouldn't remind her that the love of her life didn't want her. If someone reminded me that Rae loved Zeke more than she loved me, I wouldn't feel good about it.

"I'm gonna go," she said firmly. "I just hope something good comes out of it. At the bare minimum, I'm sure he'll leave me alone."

"And if he doesn't, I'll take care of it." I might not be her real boyfriend, but I would still do a damn good job of looking out for her. "Did he ask about me when you two were talking?"

"I told him you were my boyfriend."

"And did he have anything to say to that?"

"He seemed surprised, but no, he didn't have anything to say."

I guess I was hoping for more. I was hoping for jealousy or anger, not that it made any real difference. After all, our relationship wasn't real. It was just a hoax. The fucking and the passion were real, but all the emotions underneath that were nonexistent.

"Did Liam say anything?"

Her words dragged me from my thoughts. "He asked me if I was seeing you, and I said I was posing as your boyfriend. I said we were good friends who spent time together. I think he picked up on what I was saying."

"And he was fine with that?" she asked in surprise.

"He told me to be good to you, but that was it. Then we talked about sports."

She chuckled in a sarcastic way. "Wow. I guess I'm not surprised."

"Are you disappointed?" I asked with a raised eyebrow.

"No…a little. I mean, I don't want to have an older, protective brother. But, it doesn't really seem like he cares. If some cunt left him the way Nathan left me, you bet your ass I'd slug her in the face. But Liam saw him for the first time at the wedding and didn't seem to care."

"Maybe because he didn't want to embarrass you and cause a scene."

"No, he just isn't emotionally invested. And that's fine. That's just how we are. I'm not going to complain. I'm lucky I have a brother at all."

Rae always complained about Rex being up in her business, but now that I'd experienced siblings less involved in each other's lives, I realized Rae really did have a good thing. She was close with her brother. They were closer than family—if such a thing existed. Rex would do anything for her—in a heartbeat. "What do you mean you're lucky to have a brother at all?"

"Well…" She finished her mimosa then left the empty glass at the end of the table so the waiter knew she needed a refill. "I'm guessing Liam never told you, but…I'm adopted."

The words hit me in the face, but they didn't sink into my brain. I immediately thought of the night I met her. Liam told me she was an MIT graduate, and when I laid eyes on her, I noticed she looked nothing like Liam. They had nothing in common, not even their features. Now that she'd shared this truth with me, I realized it made complete sense. "No…he didn't mention it."

"My adoptive parents took me in when I was eleven. Before that, I lived in a foster home."

From what I knew about her, she didn't seem to have a rough upbringing. She was so soft around the edges, so happy and uplifting. Never once did I wonder if she struggled with any kind of hardship. I just assumed she was a beautiful genius who had it easy in life. I couldn't have been more wrong. "Wow…what happened to your parents?"

"My mom died in childbirth, so my dad kept me until I was about two. But then he realized he didn't want to raise a baby without my mom…so he gave me away." She spoke easily, like we were discussing something less intense than her childhood. "I never found out who he was or how I could track him down. He made sure all his information was hidden."

Now I really felt like an asshole for what I'd just said to her. "I'm sorry."

She shrugged. "My adoptive parents are great. I honestly couldn't ask for better folks to raise me. They've given me everything I needed, you know, emotionally. I know they love me like their own. But I've always suspected Liam always sees me as…his adopted sister. Not as his blood sister."

"He speaks very highly of you. I know he cares about you."

"Of course he does," she said quickly. "I'm not saying he doesn't. But…" She looked out the window again as she rubbed her lips together. "I just know if I were his real blood relative, he would be different with me. I can't really explain it, but I know it's true. And that's fine. I know I can't change the way he feels."

Now that I knew this information, I understood what she was talking about. Liam's indifference toward my seeing his sister seemed a little too laid-back for me. And the fact that he didn't care about seeing Nathan at the wedding was also alarming. I wanted to tell her she was wrong, but I couldn't do that without lying. "I'm sorry. I wish I had something better to say, but I don't."

"I know, Ryker." She gave me a slight smile. "Underneath all the ruggedness, the amazing sex, and the bossiness, you're a big sweetheart."

My mouth automatically fell into a smile. "I don't know about that...but thank you."

"Rae is stupid for choosing that other guy. I'm sure she'll regret it someday."

She wouldn't. I could tell her decision was set in stone. The time they spent together when I walked obviously impacted her life in a tremendous way. Zeke must have said all the right things, must have done all the things to win her heart. They'd been friends for so long that it wasn't surprising. He knew her better than I did—that was certain. "She won't. That's fine. I want her to be happy...even if it's not with me." Now I looked out the window, feeling as miserable as she did across the table.

We were both broken people, carrying the shards of broken hearts in our pockets. Maybe that was why we got along so well. We saw ourselves in each other, saw the misery reflected in our eyes. I didn't have to explain myself to her because she completely understood how I felt. We'd both been betrayed by the loves of our lives. It was something

that neither one of us could get over, so we clung to
each other to feel better—for as long as we could.

Chapter Sixteen

Austen

I could hardly breathe I was so nervous.

Why was I doing this?

Was this a mistake?

Should I just turn around while there was still time?

My heart wouldn't slow down.

My hands were sweaty as I gripped my clutch. I was almost to the windows of the restaurant when I stopped myself and stared at the road. Taxis and cars drove by, their lights bright now that the sunset had disappeared. My throat was dry, and my stomach was tight with unease.

It would be easy for me to walk away. All I had to do was wave down a cab and disappear. But then I would return to this moment some other time. Nathan would catch me off guard when I least expected it, outside my apartment or when I left work. At least now I knew it was coming.

If I left now, I would regret it.

So I straightened my posture and entered the restaurant, my fearless look back on my face. A part of me wanted to run to Ryker's apartment and get lost in the amazing sex we had. He'd become my rock, my home. But I knew he couldn't fix all of me—just how I couldn't fix him.

The host directed me to the table where Nathan was already sitting, wearing a collared shirt and a tie. His blond hair was styled nicely, and he greeted me with warm eyes that I hadn't seen in a long time. He looked at me like I was his world, just the way he did when he got down on one knee and asked me to marry him.

He rose from his chair to greet me, but I quickly sat down to avoid the hug.

He lowered himself back into the chair, letting the cold brush-off slide. Bread was on the table, and there was a bottle of wine, a Pinot Grigio.

I was surprised he remembered I preferred white over red.

My mouth was still parched, so I quickly looked at my menu and tried to appear calm and collected—even though I was having a mini panic attack. "What's good here?"

"I've gotten the rib eye a few times. Pretty good." Nathan didn't dive right into the conversation, which I appreciated. "But I know the prime rib is the best. They're voted the number one spot for prime rib in Manhattan."

"Thanks for the tip. I think I'll get that."

"Good choice."

I set the menu down then realized I shouldn't have made my decision so quickly. Now there was nothing to look at except his handsome face. He had kind eyes, which were innately deceitful since he'd hurt me so much. His chin was shaved, the way I preferred. He stared at me like he could hardly believe I was across from him.

I drank my wine just so I had something to do.

"What did you do today?" he asked, doing his best to break the ice.

"Ryker and I went to brunch." I wasn't going to lie just to make Nathan feel more comfortable. "Then we watched a movie."

He nodded, the kindness in his look fading. "What movie did you watch?"

I didn't expect him to ask that. "I'm not sure. We didn't watch much of it." I drank my wine again, not caring about the cold jab I just made.

Nathan slowly nodded his head, knowing he deserved that in addition to all the other insults I paid him.

"What did you do?" It was a pathetic attempt to make nice. I felt a little guilty for being a bitch to him...even though he deserved it.

"I went for a jog in the park. Then I stayed home all day."

"Where's your apartment?"

"On 8th and Elm."

That was a nice side of town. He was probably still in the graphic section of the marketing department. He was an artistic director, overseeing all ads in mainstream media. We had a lot in common because our jobs were similar. "That sounds nice."

"You like being back in the city?"

"So far, I love it. It's nice to see Liam and my parents more often. And Ryker is a native, so he's taken me to some cool places."

He paled at the mention of Ryker again. "What does he do?"

"Nothing."

"Nothing?" He couldn't hide his surprise.

"He's wealthy. Invested his fortune and now he kicks back." I wouldn't call him lazy. You couldn't be lazy and make a retirement at such a young age.

"He seemed like the rich type."

I gave him a warning with my eyes, telling him he would be stupid to insult the man I was sleeping with. Ryker was important to me. He made me feel good when no one else could. He was honest, good, and a big sweetheart underneath all that coldness.

Nathan made the right decision and remained quiet.

The waiter came over and took our orders then walked away again.

Now we were back to the awkwardness. Since the pleasantries were out of the way and there was no more small talk to make, there was nothing left to do but have the conversation we'd agreed to have.

"Nathan, what did you want to tell me?" I tried not to get my hopes up. I doubted there was anything he could really say to give me closure. It'd been too long since we'd broken up. I was probably too fucked up to be fixed at this point.

He sighed quietly before he took a drink of his wine, steeling himself before he spoke. He rested his elbows on the table and leaned forward, his eyes glued to mine and no one else's. "First of all, thank you for having dinner with me—"

"Don't kiss my ass. Just get on with it."

He pressed his lips tightly together as he absorbed the command. It took him a moment to keep talking like nothing happened. "Do you want to know how it happened? How it started?"

"I guess."

"Okay. I went out with Adam and Roger. We went to that bar around the corner from our apartment. I was drinking a lot. The Mets just won the World Series, so I was drinking far more than I should. I went to the bathroom, ran into Lily, and…the rest is a little blurry. She kissed me, and I kissed her back. Things heated up, and there was touching. We ended up in the bathroom together…and that was the first time I slept with her."

I thought this information wouldn't hurt me since it happened so long ago. But I was wrong. It hurt like fucking hell. Picturing them together, making out and touching each other…it made me regret ordering the prime rib.

"I felt guilty for what I did—truly."

I stopped myself from rolling my eyes.

"I debated how I was going to tell you. I knew I was going to come clean about it, but I hadn't found the courage to do it. I loved you, and I didn't want to ruin what we had. So I kept waiting…waiting for the right moment."

"And then you fell in love with her instead?"

"No," he said quickly. "She and I talked about that night. I told her I wasn't going to tell you anything. It only happened one time, and it didn't mean anything. Plus, since it was Lily, I knew it would ruin your friendship...no good could come from it."

Now I did roll my eyes.

"But she said she would tell you what was going on unless I slept with her again..."

"What?" I couldn't stop my outburst from exploding. "Are you serious?"

He nodded. "She said she wanted to hook up again. If I didn't do what she wanted, she was going to tell you everything. But she was going to tell you a different version of what really happened, that I came on to her and we'd been sleeping together for months... I didn't know what to do, so I did as she asked."

I couldn't believe Lily did that to me. We'd been friends since we braided each other's hair for the first time in sixth grade. We did everything together. We were inseparable until we went to different colleges. I never did anything to her to deserve this nightmare. "I can't believe that..."

"I'm not making it up. The fact that Lily hasn't spoken to you in three years is proof enough."

He was right about that. I never understood how we were so close then she ran off with my fiancé. It was like she was a different person.

"Of course, that one time turned into two. Then it turned into three, and it just kept going. I got fed up with it and told her I didn't care anymore. She could tell you the truth for all I cared."

"And then what happened?" Now I was invested in the story, needing to know what happened even though I already lived through the nightmare.

"She told me she was pregnant."

I shut my mouth and clenched my jaw, thinking about Lily pregnant with Nathan's child. He and I were the ones who were supposed to get married and have children. But she decided to sabotage that.

I knew they never had children. If they had, I would have known about it. So something must have happened.

"When she told me she was pregnant, I knew I was screwed. I was in too deep, and I couldn't fix our relationship. I knew there was no other outcome for us besides a breakup. I mean, it never would have worked. So…that was why I left. I asked her to marry me because I wanted to be a family. We had great sex, and we did get along well…" He didn't make eye contact with me when he said that part. "So I just bit the bullet and did it. But then she told me she lost the baby, which was probably a lie. She probably was never pregnant to begin with. But we were married, and I thought we could make it work. She was a lot different after we tied the knot. Affectionate, loving, friendly…we had good times. But I got to the end of the road and knew I couldn't do it for the rest of my life. I made a stupid mistake, but I didn't deserve to be punished forever. So I left her." He watched me across the table, his eyes taking in my reaction. "And now I'm here with you."

He could tell me that story a million times, but I would never be able to digest it. It left a bad taste in my mouth, a disgusting sensation. "There's something that's not making any sense…"

"I'll tell you anything you want to know." He jumped at the possibility of making things easier for me, but there was nothing he could do to erase the last three years of anguish.

"Why did Lily do this to me? It seemed like revenge."

He nodded like he expected me to ask that. "I didn't get the truth out of her for a while. Apparently, she found out that you slept with Owen

Carter when you knew she was in love with him. She found out from Cassandra Taylor..."

I slept with Owen when I was in college, and it was a stupid mistake. I was drunk and he was drunk. I knew she had feelings for him, but they weren't even seeing each other. They hadn't even been on a first date. I felt terrible for what I did, and I planned to take the secret to my grave. Owen must have told Cassandra, who then told Lily a few years later. "That's the dumbest thing I've ever heard."

He shrugged. "I thought it was extreme too."

"I'm not making excuses for what I did. It was really terrible. I was a shitty friend. But they weren't even seeing each other. She just said she really liked him, but he never asked her out. And I didn't plan on sleeping with him. It just—"

"I know. I'm totally on your side, Austen."

"And to steal the love of my life...that's just low. Those aren't even comparable crimes."

His eyes softened at my words.

I wished I hadn't said that, but now it was too late. I pushed through like it never happened. "I can't believe all of this happened because of something like Owen Carter..."

"Lily has always been the petty type. She's vain, selfish... You just never noticed because she was on your team. When you guys are on the same side, she's an angel. But that doesn't mean she's not a little crazy."

I knew all of that was true since he was married to her.

"I still don't know why you didn't tell me any of this when you left."

He stared at the table for a long time like he didn't know how to answer. "So much had happened…so many terrible things. When I saw the look on your face when you caught us together…there was no going back. Nothing I said was going to make the situation better. Saying nothing and just leaving you alone was the best thing I could do for you."

After all this time, after all these years of heartbreak, this was the truth. "Nathan, I would have appreciated knowing what really happened. I was going to marry you. I think I deserved the truth, even if we couldn't get back together."

"I know." He bowed his head. "You're right. That's why I'm here now."

It was too late.

"I know I didn't really fix anything. But I wanted you to know that I didn't leave because I was unhappy with you or because I wasn't in love with you. I left because…I was a fucking idiot and got myself mixed up with stupidity. I missed you a lot. I tried to love Lily, and I eventually grew fond of her…but she was never you."

The tears started deep inside my chest, but I never let them progress up my throat. I couldn't let Nathan see my tears—not now or ever. This conversation gave me closure, which was I grateful for. But it somehow made me feel worse. If Lily hadn't struck a vendetta against me, I could be happy right now. I could be married and surrounded by my children.

"I'm so sorry, Austen." He blinked away the moisture that formed in his eyes. "If I could take it back, I would. I wish we were in living in a house in the country. I wish our kids were three years old and walking. I wish…I wish everything was different."

"And I wish you hadn't slept with her in that bar," I said coldly. "Lily is to blame for a lot of this, but none of it would have happened if you hadn't fucked her, Nathan. You could have just walked away, no matter how drunk you were. That will never be a suitable excuse."

He didn't argue. "You're right. I shouldn't have let it happen. I shouldn't have drunk that much. I should have done whatever it took to get the hell out of there and back to you. Believe me, not a day goes by that I don't regret that god-awful night." He covered his face with his hands and slowly dragged them down his cheeks. He released a quiet sigh, showing a broken and vulnerable side that I hadn't noticed until now. "I know sorry isn't good enough. It'll never be good enough. But believe me when I say, I hate myself for what I've done to you. Not just then, but the years in between. It was wrong of me ever to let you think I stopped loving you...because I never stopped." He looked me in the eye again, his eyes wet. "I'll never stop."

My heart slammed in my chest, racing a million miles a minute. I could hardly breathe because everything was working in overdrive. Nathan just poured his heart out in the middle of dinner, and I actually believed his confession of remorse. My hatred for him ebbed away because I couldn't hold on to it any longer. "I forgive you, Nathan."

He stared at me with hollow eyes, like he couldn't believe me.

"Truly. I do."

"Austen...you give me more compassion than I deserve."

Maybe letting go would finally free me from my own torture. Maybe I could trust a man again. Maybe I could have a real relationship that wasn't solely based on sex. Maybe I had a chance at real happiness. "I don't want to keep hating you. I want to move on with my life. I think I can do that now."

He brought his hands together on the table. His shoulders looked broad and powerful in the collared shirt. He was just as in shape as he'd always been. A good-looking guy like him could find someone to settle down with in a heartbeat. "I know I'm pushing my luck right now. But…I would really love another chance to be with you. I know I don't deserve you, not after what I did. But…I know you still love me. And I still love you. What happened to us was a tragedy. We have to fix it. We have to have the life we were meant to live."

Deep in my gut, I suspected this was his motive all along. I couldn't count the number of fantasies I'd had about this moment. I pictured him saying Lily wasn't half the woman I was and he'd made the worst mistake of his life by being with her. He was on his hands and knees, begging for another opportunity. But those fantasies died a year after we broke up. But then, I knew he wasn't coming back. "No."

Disappointment rose into his features. "I was expecting you to say that. Can we do baby steps? Will you have coffee with me on Tuesday?"

"I don't want to do baby steps, Nathan."

"But you love me." He said it with more confidence than I'd ever heard him utter. "I can see it in your eyes."

My feelings were undeniable, even to me. I wouldn't be sitting at that table with him if feelings weren't there. I wouldn't have been single for the past few years if I was really over him. I wouldn't be doing half the things I did if I was really okay. I knew I wanted to be with him, to have the beautiful relationship we once had. But love wasn't enough for me. "I do." I didn't feel ashamed for admitting it. It was obvious Nathan knew the truth anyway. "But it'll never work. I don't trust you, and I never will. And without trust...there's nothing there."

"I can earn your trust, Austen. It'll take time, but I can do it."

"Besides, I'm seeing someone." Ryker popped into my mind. I wondered what he would say once I told him about my evening.

"I know you don't love him."

"That doesn't matter." Maybe I wasn't in love with him, but I did care for him—a lot. He'd become my best friend over the past few months. We did almost everything together, developing a beautiful camaraderie we both enjoyed. We were two broken people who fit together perfectly.

Nathan sighed like he'd given up the argument. Or perhaps he just postponed it for another time. "Thank you for having dinner with me. I've wanted to get this off my chest for a long time."

I didn't have the will to say anything back, to say something positive to make the conversation less stressful. Knowing the truth made things easier, and forgiving him allowed my body to finally relax. But no matter what pretty words he said to me, it wouldn't change the fact that he broke my heart.

Chapter Seventeen

Ryker

I tried to keep myself busy so I wouldn't think about Austen. I did the dishes, folded some laundry, and then watched the game on TV with a cold beer sitting on my knee. But my thoughts trailed to her anyway.

I eyed the time, wondering if her dinner was finished yet. I wanted to ask her how it went, if that piece of shit managed to say something to make her forgive him. I sincerely hoped not. The second I looked at him, I didn't like him. It ticked me off that he kept hunting down Austen like he was entitled to her time.

When ten o'clock came and went, I started to get worried. Did they make up and now she was going back to his place? I knew Austen well enough to know that was extremely unlikely. Even though she still had feelings for him, she wouldn't sell herself short like that. She was better than that.

But that didn't stop me from stressing out.

When I couldn't take it anymore, I caved. I texted her. *How'd it go?*

The three little dots didn't show up on the screen. Her message box was completely empty. I wanted to say something else, but that would make me look like a clingy weirdo. I shouldn't have texted her to begin with. If she wanted to talk about it, she would have called me.

But I kept glancing at my phone anyway, hoping for those three little dots.

There was nothing.

I started to get worked up all over again, thinking about their clothes falling into a pile on the floor. I pictured his hands all over her body, his lips treasuring her skin like she was his again.

I nearly crushed my bottle in my hand.

Finally, the three dots appeared.

Thank fucking god.

Can't really answer that through a text message.

Then come over. I wanted her here anyway. If she was with me, then she wasn't with him.

I'm on my way.

I cleaned up the apartment and tossed my beer because I wasn't in the mood to drink anything. I was just anxious to hear her story, to know what happened between them over dinner.

She finally walked inside, looking stunning in the black cocktail dress she wore with heels. There was no way he sat across from her at the table and didn't think about fucking her.

My arms circled her waist, and I brought her into my chest, cradling her like a gentle flower. I kissed her because my mouth was so eager for hers.

She kissed me like she always did, with the same eagerness and affection.

Once my lips and hands touched her, my natural instinct was to head to the bedroom and move between her legs. That was the way we communicated—with our bodies. My hands gripped the fabric of her dress but refrained from yanking it over her hips. I finally pulled away and looked at her. Her expression wasn't easy to read like it usually was. Now I was in the dark, unsure what she was feeling. "What happened, sweetheart?"

She told me everything Nathan told her, that he didn't leave because he wanted to. He was essentially blackmailed because of one stupid mistake that he made. Then the hole he stood in got deeper and more complicated. It tore their relationship apart. "He seemed sincere about the whole thing. I don't think he's lying."

I couldn't believe Austen had a friend who would do that to her. She was so nice and loyal to her girlfriends. She didn't deserve that. "Lily needs to get her ass kicked."

"She'll get what's coming to her. Karma works that way."

"Yeah, you're probably right." I ran my hands up and down her arms, being as emotionally available as possible. "You didn't deserve that after sleeping with Owen. That was totally blown out of proportion."

She rolled her eyes. "Tell me about it..."

"Anything else happen?" Nathan must have had another motive to sit down with her and confess the truth. He had years to do it, but he waited until now. The reason was pretty obvious to me.

"He asked for another chance."

I held her gaze as I waited for her response. Even with the explanation, his behavior was inexcusable. That hookup in the bar never should have happened, not when he had a beautiful woman waiting for him at home. But I didn't tell her that because she already knew my opinion about the matter.

"I said no."

I tried to mask my relief as much as possible. I wanted to sigh, but I stopped myself from doing it and giving away my feelings.

"Now that I know what really happened, I feel better. I guess knowing it was much more complicated than him simply falling in love with someone else makes things easier. It wasn't because of me. It wasn't my fault."

"Of course it wasn't your fault. You shouldn't have even thought that to begin with."

She shrugged and looked away. "After he left me, I swore off men for the rest of my life. I wanted to be alone forever, never trusting anyone. But now this gives me hope. Maybe I can get better and be normal again."

I didn't want her to be normal again. I wanted her to stay broken just like me, as selfish as that was. "Even if he never told you the truth, not all men are like that, Austen. There are plenty of men who are honest, faithful, and extremely loyal. Don't let one bad one ruin your opinion of the rest."

"I know..."

"I'm glad you didn't give him another chance." Since she'd already made her decision, I didn't feel guilty for saying it. "You deserve someone better than that, someone who can get their shit right the first time around."

She gave me a weak smile, the kind that was forced. "Thanks, Ryker. You're always so sweet to me."

"Not true and you know it." I moved into her and cupped her cheeks with my hands. My fingers touched her soft hair, and I inhaled her scent. "You know I'm rough and mean when we're naked together. But you like it like that."

Her hands wrapped around my wrists, and she gave me an affectionate look. "I do."

I pressed my mouth to hers and kissed her, adoring her soft lips as they moved against mine. My fingers dug into her neck, and I felt my desperation creep to the surface. My need grew in intensity until my breathing grew deep and rugged. I wanted to be buried inside her, but now it was for a different reason.

I wanted her to be mine.

***

"Damn, that woman is fine." John nodded across the bar to a woman in a tight black dress. She had blond hair and blue eyes, looking like a Barbie doll.

I glanced in her direction then turned back to him. "Did you see the game last night. I can't believe—"

"That's it? You aren't impressed?"

"Impressed by what?" I drank my beer as I stared at him, unsure what he was talking about.

"I said that woman was hot, and you changed the subject to sports."

"What do you want me to say?" I countered. "She's hot. So what?" There were beautiful women all over the city at any given time. If you tried to look at them all, you were going to get serious neck cramps.

Liam returned from the end of the bar with a new beer in hand. "It's because he's seeing my sister." He stood between us and eyed the people having a good time under the dim lighting. "He's tied down at the moment."

"You're tapping Austen?" John asked in surprise.

I immediately turned angry once he talked about Austen like she was some kind of piece of ass. "Don't talk about her like that."

"Ooh…there's my answer," John said with a laugh. "How long has this been going on?"

"We aren't seeing each other," I corrected. "We just hang out. That's all." I kept it PG, even though Liam didn't seem to care either way.

"Until she breaks your heart like all the others," Liam said. "Give it time."

"She's not gonna break my heart." I didn't have a heart to break. Rae did a pretty good job of ruining me for the rest of my life. "And I'm not going to break hers. We're really good friends."

"You mean, you're really good fuck buddies," John corrected.

I glared at him again. "If you don't want a broken jaw tonight, I suggest you watch what you say."

"What?" John asked innocently. "Are you saying I'm wrong?"

No. He hit the nail right on the head. "Just don't talk about Austen like that. If you can't do that, then don't talk about her at all."

Liam eyed me with a concentrated stare. He held his beer but didn't take a drink, focused on my reaction. He exchanged a look with John before he looked at me again. "Ryker...do you have feelings for my sister?"

"I wouldn't be hanging out with her if I didn't," I snapped.

"But like, real feelings," Liam said. "It almost seems like—"

"We're really good friends." I wanted this interrogation to end then and there. "Yes, you're right." I downed my beer then silently excused myself to the restroom, wanting to avoid their idiotic assumptions and questions.

I walked into the hallway where the bathrooms were located and pulled out my phone. *What are you doing?* I fired off the message instantly and watched the dots appear.

Eating a slice of greasy ass pizza.

I immediately smiled, like the guys didn't just piss me off. *Sounds hot.*

I'm pretty much making love to it.

I chuckled out loud without caring if anyone saw me. *I'm so hard right now.*

The sad thing is, I'm not sure if you're joking.

Well, I am always hard when it comes to you. You'll never know until you check yourself.

I'm out with Mad and Jenn right now, so I'm not sure if I can make that happen.

How long will you be out with them?

Who knows? There's been talk of going racing.

Racing?

At an indoor track with electric cars.

I smiled because the idea of her racing in a little car was adorable. *Now that's really hot.*

You guys wanna come?

I definitely didn't want to hang out at this bar and check out the women hanging around. They were just blurs to me. Why would I pick up a woman when I already had a fine little number I could call at any time? *I'll check with the guys. Our evening is pretty boring, so they'll probably say yes.*

Where are you?

At a bar.

No sexy ladies?

None that I can see. I shoved my phone into my pocket and walked back to the guys at the bar. "You guys wanna go racing with the girls? They're heading to a track with electric cars."

"Madeline gonna be there?" Liam blurted.

"Yep. So is Jenn," I answered.

"Ooh...Jenn is hot." John downed the rest of his glass and set it on the counter and tossed the cash on the table. "Let's go."

We left the bar then walked up the sidewalk, passing other New Yorkers as we went. "What's happening with you and Madeline?" I couldn't tell if they were exclusive or not. He didn't hit on other women, but he was still checking them out.

"Went on a few dates." Liam walked with his hands in his pockets. "Taking it slow. Don't want to scare her off."

"Don't play games either," I said. "If you like the woman, just tell her."

"You're one to talk," he said with a laugh.

"What's that supposed to mean?" I stared at him as we walked.

"You're so sprung off Austen. You guys aren't just casual friends. I warned you about her, but you didn't listen to me." He shook his head in disappointment.

"We are just casual friends." When we started fooling around, I didn't expect it to last this long. And I didn't expect to be so fond of her. But I found myself wanting to spend time with her even when sex wasn't involved. But that didn't mean my feelings were anything less than superficial.

"You didn't even look at that woman in the bar," Liam argued.

"Because she wasn't that pretty," I countered. "That's all."

Liam clearly didn't believe me. "Do what you want, alright? It doesn't make a difference to me either way. But be honest about it. If you aren't, you're gonna get your heart stomped on. Don't say I didn't warn you."

"Thanks for the warning," I said sarcastically. "I forgot your sister is such a monster."

"She's not a monster," Liam argued. "She's just a heartbreaker. Plain and simple."

I'd been seeing her for almost three months, and I didn't get that vibe from her whatsoever. She was harmless and honest. She met with Nathan and even forgave him. A cold person would never do that.

"You're my friend, and I don't want you to get hurt," Liam said. "That's all. I think you're falling for her, and you don't even realize it."

"Trust me, I'm not falling for her." Rae was still on my mind almost every day. I wanted her face to disappear from my dreams. I wanted her presence to disappear from my heart. She was happy with another man, and I needed to move on with my life.

"Whatever you say, man."

We arrived at the racetrack and paid to get in. The girls were already there, sitting at a table sharing a plate of nachos. Their helmets were set on the surface, large racing helmets the pros used.

I wanted to laugh when I pictured Austen wearing one.

"Hey." My eyes were on Austen when I walked up to their table. "Didn't you just eat pizza?"

Austen popped a chip into her mouth before she stood up. "Yeah, but it was only one slice. And drop the judgment, alright?"

"No judgment." I smiled before I wrapped my arm around her waist and kissed her on the mouth.

She stilled at my touch like she didn't expect the affection.

I didn't even realize what I did until the damage was done. When we were around our friends, we kept our hands to ourselves. The wedding was a one-time thing. But the second I looked at her beautiful blue eyes, I lost my train of thought and reacted off instinct.

I pulled my hand from her waist and cleared my throat. "You ready to race?"

She tucked her hair behind her ear. "Yeah, definitely. I'm not gonna go easy on you though. So be prepared to get smoked."

"You're gonna kick my ass?" I smiled again when her comment broke the tension. "You just keep getting hotter and hotter."

She rolled her eyes and turned back to the group. "Let's hit the track. The losing team buys the next round."

***

The women smoked us.

Bad.

I wasn't even going to sugarcoat the defeat. It was obvious it wasn't their first time on the track.

Austen and I walked back to my apartment after we said goodbye to everyone else. "Where did you guys learn to drive like that?"

"Madeline and I have been doing it since we were kids. So don't feel bad."

Now that we were alone together, I grabbed her hand and interlocked our fingers.

She didn't tense at the touch, but she glanced down at our joined hands.

"I do feel bad. We got our asses handed to us."

"Well, practice makes perfect."

"I could practice for a year and still not be as good as you." We entered the apartment and took the elevator to my apartment. Once we were inside, we both entered the bedroom automatically. "But I'm awesome at bowling. So I'll kick your ass, then."

"I like bowling."

Now that we were alone together, my hands immediately went for her clothes. I held her gaze as I pulled her top over her head and unclasped her bra. I'd undressed her so many times that the action was instinct. I went for her jeans next, kneeling down as I pulled them off. I kissed her legs as I pulled the jeans from her ankles, spreading soft kisses against her warm skin. I loved everything about her—particularly these gorgeous legs.

I pulled her panties off next then pressed my mouth against her nub. I kissed the delicate skin tenderly, teasing her clit until I gave her the kind of pleasure she craved. Her breathing increased, and she gripped my shoulders for balance.

I wanted to keep tasting her pussy, but my cock was hard and angry in my jeans. He was anxious to be free, to fuck this woman with all the aggression built up inside him. I rose to my feet then positioned her at the foot of the bed. I liked taking her like this because I could get deep inside her, giving her every single inch of my cock with every stroke.

I dropped my jeans and boxers but left my shirt on, too anxious to care about getting naked. I rubbed my length over her wet pussy, lubricating myself and playing with her throbbing clit. Then I shoved myself inside her, feeling the slickness I was used to.

It felt incredible.

We both inhaled together, our quiet moans tangled. My hand moved behind her knees, and her hands gripped my wrists. I thrust into her slowly, taking my time to enjoy her phenomenal pussy. Every time I was inside her, I felt more like a man than I did before. "Austen..." I leaned over her and moved my chest against hers. "This pussy..."

She craned her neck so her lips could reach mine. She kissed me with her soft lips, her tongue meeting mine. "I'm in love with your cock..." Her tongue darted into my mouth, tasting like tequila.

I moaned into her mouth as I moved, giving it to her harder and deeper. She knew exactly what to say to get me worked up. My head moved in and out, soaked with her arousal. I could feel it every time I moved, to sense her powerful desire. One thing I loved about being a man was making a woman wet. I got to directly reap the benefits, and she got to have an incredible orgasm.

I spoke against her mouth. "I already want to come..." She tested my endurance. She was so sexy, so perfect, that I couldn't hold my concentration. The moment I was inside her, I didn't want to last. I wanted to explode and feel the fiery explosion deep inside my gut.

"Come." She tightened her grip on my wrists. "We'll keep going anyway."

When she gave me her explicit permission, I couldn't hold on. I always made my women come first, but I knew it was one of those nights when we wouldn't be getting any sleep. It wasn't a quick fuck before bed. It was the beginning of a long night.

She gripped my ass and pulled me deep inside her, a heated look in her eyes. Her nipples were hard and pointed to the ceiling, and her pussy was tight around my cock. "Give it to me, Ryker."

I couldn't last any longer, not when she gave me a command like that. Balls deep, I released with a groan, dumping all of my seed far inside her pussy. I breathed through the explicit pleasure, feeling the sensation move from the tip of my cock to deep within my balls. "Fuck..."

Her eyes darkened as she watched me come, her tongue darting out and licking her lips. She moved her hands across my stomach and up my chest. "You look so sexy when you come..."

"Yeah?" My cock slowly softened inside her, but I still felt the high from my orgasm. I was satisfied but also eager for more at the same time. I moved my hips and continued to rock inside her even though my cock was no longer hard. With that look in her eyes and the feeling of her drenched pussy, I would be hard again within two minutes.

Austen began to play with her tits, flicking her thumb over her nipples then leaning down to lick them.

That sped up the process.

I was harder than I was before and motivated to make her feel as good as I did. "That pussy isn't going to be able to hold all my come by the time I'm done with you."

"I expected nothing less."

Chapter Eighteen

Austen

When I got off work, I thought about going to the gym. I hadn't been in a while, and I really needed to get my butt into gear. I had a treadmill desk so I didn't sit in a chair all day long, but that still didn't get my heart rate up. But I was a pretty lazy person. The gym was exhausting and boring at the same time—not my style.

Besides, Ryker certainly got my heart rate up.

I walked out of the office and took the elevator to the lobby, feeling guilty for not changing into my gym clothes. I left the bag in my office just in case I changed my mind tomorrow—which was extremely unlikely.

I finally walked out of the building and directly into the sunshine. Instead of enjoying the beautiful day and the sweltering heat, I nearly walked right into Nathan. "Geez, you scared the crap out of me." I stepped back with my hand over my chest, not expecting him to appear out of nowhere like that.

"Sorry." He stepped back like distance would make this situation better. "I was just passing by on my way to the store. Wasn't expecting to see you."

I saw right through that. I gave him a look that said I was calling him out on his bullshit.

"Okay…maybe I wasn't going to the store."

Now that Nathan and I had had dinner together, I wasn't repulsed by him. I could look at him without insulting him. The rage I once possessed was gone. I would even go far enough to say I was actually calm around him.

"I was going to grab a coffee from The Muffin Girl. You wanna join?"

He'd asked me to give him another chance, and I said no. Perhaps he wasn't accepting my answer. "We're never getting back together, Nathan. I don't want you to waste your time."

"That's fine," he said quickly. "But can we be friends? You were a big part of my life, Austen. I know I was a big part of yours. It would be a shame if we couldn't preserve something, right?"

The suggestion seemed harmless, but I'd been tricked before.

"It's just coffee. Nice conversation."

When he made it sound so easy, I couldn't turn him down. His five o'clock shadow had come in, and he'd done his hair that day. He looked handsome in the t-shirt he wore, his lean muscles and strong frame filling out the fabric well. I suspected I would always be attracted to him, always have a spot for him. "Uh, okay."

He beamed like it was the happiest day of his life. "Awesome."

***

We got our coffees and muffins and sat at a picnic table outside. Nathan didn't try to pay for my food, for which I was grateful. Anytime a man offered to pay, it made it seem like a date.

And this definitely wasn't a date.

At first, it was awkward to sit across from one another. I set my phone on the surface just in case someone texted me. And by someone, I meant Ryker. I saw him almost every single day. That was the norm for us now. I picked at my blueberry muffin, taking small bites just so I had something to do other than stare at him.

"How was your day?" he asked.

"Good. I just launched this new marketing campaign that seems to be working. My boss said he's pleased with it."

"I'm sure it'll be great. You're a genius when it comes to stuff like that."

Controlling the narrative and the perspective of the general population was a strained art. It was too difficult to predict how people would receive advertisements and news. But that was why I loved it so much. It was wild and uncontrollable. "I do my best and hope for a good reaction. When it comes to the area of social media, you never know what's gonna happen."

"I can imagine."

"How's Helium?" Nathan worked as an art director for an online streaming service where people watched TV shows and movies directly in their homes.

"The same. We've been producing more than ever, so we've hired some new talent. We've got so many ads running I can't even keep track anymore. I just designed a billboard. It's over on Houston."

"Oh, that's cool." I worked with an art director on a daily basis to get what we needed. It was ironic that Nathan and I had so much in common professionally. We really were a great couple. There wasn't a single thing I would have changed about our relationship while we were together.

"I have to work more when I'd rather not, but that's okay. I love my job."

I nodded in agreement because I loved mine too. There was nothing else I'd rather be doing. I sipped my coffee and glanced at my phone, hoping a message from Ryker would pop up. I couldn't leave Nathan so quickly, but I was still eager to get to Ryker's apartment to do what we did best.

"How are the girls? I didn't get a chance to speak to them at the wedding."

Good thing he didn't try. Maddie probably would have punched him. "Good. Looks like Maddie is seeing my brother. I hope that doesn't go to shit."

"Yeah, that could get complicated."

"Jared is seeing this nice girl, but I can tell he's still into Maddie. I catch him looking at her all the time." I wasn't sure why I was telling Nathan this. I fell back into our old ways when I told him all the insignificant details of my life. It was frightening how easily it happened, like I just came home from work and we were telling each other about our day.

"Can't blame him. She's a catch."

I didn't feel the surge of jealousy like I thought I might. Madeline would never backstab me the way Lily did, so there was no reason to be upset by his comment. Besides, he was right. He would have to be blind not to find her attractive.

"But I feel bad for the girl he's seeing. That's not fair to her."

He was one to talk.

Nathan caught on to my change of mood. "It's okay to still be angry at me. You have every right to be."

After all this time, he still knew me so well. "Do you have any roommates?" It was a stupid question and I didn't even care about the answer, but I asked it just to change the subject.

"No. I'm alone in a one-bedroom apartment. I'm too old for a roommate. Wouldn't have the patience for it."

I didn't want a roommate either. After sharing an apartment all through college, I was over it. I'd rather pay the extra cash for my privacy. I was still saving money, just not as much as I could be saving.

"Do anything fun last night?"

"We went racing."

"Like go-carts?" he asked.

"No. The cars are actually pretty fast. You have to wear helmets and everything."

"Sounds intense."

"The girls and I won. Totally smoked the guys."

He wore a forced smile, probably assuming Ryker was there. "You should go pro."

"Nah," I said as I picked at my muffin again. "I'll crash and kill lots of people."

He chuckled. "Then you should definitely stay off the racetrack." He sipped his coffee and eyed the café through the window. His eyes stayed there for a long time before he turned back to me. "How are your folks?"

I assumed he would ask about them eventually. "Good. Still live at the edge of the city."

"Cool." Nathan and my father used to be close. They went fishing a few times. He never saw my parents again after he left me.

Both of my parents were pissed when they found out what happened, but they never showed it around me, probably knowing it would only make me feel worse. My parents were selfless like that. "My dad just got a new BBQ. So he's been grilling all summer."

"That sounds nice."

"He knows how to prepare a great burger. When he retires, I think he should have his own cooking show."

"I'd watch that," he said with a smile.

"How are your parents?"

"They're good. Mom is still an interior decorator. She likes it. My dad loves being retired."

"Cool. And your brother?"

"He's the same knucklehead he's always been," he said with a chuckle. "He's still at Dynamite Fitness around the corner."

"Still a personal trainer?"

"Yep." He nodded. "Still ripped as hell."

"Well, you're pretty ripped too." The words tumbled out of my mouth like vomit, and I immediately regretted saying them. It was obvious I was attracted to him because I did agree to marry him at one point, but I didn't want to wear my feelings on my sleeve. I learned my lesson the hard way.

"Thanks. You look like you're in shape too."

I laughed because he couldn't be more wrong. "I've been trying to talk myself into going to the gym every single day after work…but I never go."

"Good. We wouldn't be having coffee together if you did."

I forced my cheeks not to blush. I wasn't sure how I did it, but I managed to make it happen. "Good thing you aren't a personal trainer. I don't think you'd be very good at it."

He chuckled. "You have a good point."

I finished the rest of my muffin then had nothing else to pick at except the wrapper. For the entire conversation, I had my guard up and refused to let him in. The trust was permanently broken, and nothing could repair it. But I still felt something for him. I suspected I would for the rest of my life. When I said I loved him, I really meant it. I thought he was my Prince Charming, the man I thought I was supposed to be with. Could I ever really stop loving someone I'd loved so much? I didn't think it was possible—at least not for me.

Nathan picked up on the subtle mood change. "What did I say?"

"Nothing," I said quickly. "I was just drifting for a second there..."

His eyes softened like he knew it was a lie. "I'm always here to talk if you need someone to listen—about anything. I miss our conversations over dinner. I miss telling you about my day. I miss hearing you tell me about yours. Even if we can't be together again, I would love just to talk to you. I know that sounds weird—"

"I understand, Nathan." The first year of our breakup, I wanted him to call me. I wanted something from him—anything. I managed not to reach out to him because my pride wouldn't allow me to look so weak. But I definitely thought about it a few times. "More than you know."

***

I drank a bottle of wine by myself while I sat on the couch and watched TV. A game was on, but I wasn't really watching it because I was thinking about my afternoon with Nathan.

What the hell was I doing?

How did I still have feelings for him after what he did to me?

He cheated on me.

Cheated.

I hadn't had a single relationship since that god-awful day, and I'd given up on love entirely. But all that heartbreak disappeared once I got an apology from him. I even had coffee with him when I didn't owe him a damn thing.

What was wrong with me?

I couldn't go down that road again. Nathan seemed sincere about his apology. He seemed patient and understanding. And he seemed like the man I used to know, the one who would do anything for me.

But that shouldn't be enough.

If I gave him another chance, my friends would never approve. My parents would be livid. Liam would be annoyed. No one would be on my side—except Ryker. I knew he didn't like Nathan after what he did to me, but he would accept it. No one else would.

But even if I couldn't get everyone else on board, that shouldn't matter. Nathan slept with someone else, so I could never trust him again. That wasn't how I was going to get my happily ever after. I respected myself way too much.

But then I felt that tingly sensation in my gut when I looked at him across the table. When he asked me to coffee, I couldn't say no. I found myself walking down memory lane, recalling the way he proposed to me on the sand of Myrtle Beach.

What was wrong with me?

I just finished the last drop of wine when Ryker called me. I didn't want to talk right then, but I didn't want to be alone tonight either. Whenever I was with that man, I was happy. I didn't think about my problems. I just fell into a safe place, knowing no one could ever harm me. Something about his rugged smile, his beautiful eyes, and that good heart made me forget all the bullshit in my life. Even when we weren't screwing, I was happy.

I picked up before it went to voice mail. "Hello?"

"I'll take a large combination with extra olives, please."

I raised an eyebrow, not catching on to his strange game. "Extra olives? You're greedy."

"Hey, I'll pay for the extras. So when is my delivery going to arrive? I'm starving."

My stomach rumbled because I hadn't had anything since that muffin. "Depends."

"I'll tip you real nice."

I laughed. "No. You better order a real pizza because now my stomach is rumbling."

He chuckled. "I'm on it. A combination with no onion, right?"

Ryker knew me better than I gave him credit for. "Yep."

"I'll order it now. But that doesn't mean I don't want your ass over here as soon as possible."

"Alright, my ass is coming."

"Good. See you soon, sweetheart." He hung up.

I listened to the line go dead. The second we started talking, I felt uplifted. He was the only person who could make me laugh with I was down. He was the only person who could make me feel wanted without even trying. And now I felt better. I eyed my empty bottle of wine and didn't know why I'd moped around all day in the first place. I could have just gone to his place.

I packed a bag then walked to his apartment a few blocks over. I never took a cab because they usually smelled like cigarette smoke, and they took forever to get anywhere anyway. When I walked, I got to stretch my legs and enjoy the view of Central Park along the way.

I arrived at his door fifteen minutes later, my bag over my shoulder.

The second he opened the door, he snatched me and yanked me inside. "There's my dinner." He shut the door and pressed me against it, his mouth on mine. He gave me a scorching kiss as he grabbed my hands and pinned them against the wood. He sucked my bottom lip into his mouth before he gave me some of his tongue. "Yum."

I was still starving, but I didn't care about the pizza anymore. I cared about the feast that was right before my eyes. I yanked his shirt over his head, revealing his perfectly chiseled chest and his tight stomach. "Stay just like that..." I pressed my hand against his chest and forced him to lean back slightly.

"This better be good."

I pulled my phone from my back pocket and took a picture of him, capturing his brooding gaze and his rugged jawline. His flawless physique looked even better photographed. "Perfect. That way I can see this picture every time you call me."

"And every time you touch yourself." Now that the phone was back in my pocket, he pressed his body against mine again and kissed me harder than he did before. He undid my jeans and yanked them off as I removed his. Soon, our bottoms were gone, and my body was in the air with my back against the door.

"You can't even get through the front door without being fucked." He shoved himself inside me, holding me up with ease as he kissed me again.

"Why do you think I come over all the time?"

He smiled against my mouth as he continued to thrust into me hard against the door. His hips bucked as he gave me his entire length over and over. Sweat collected on his body as he worked to please both of us, giving it to me good and hard.

It was a rough and quick fuck, both of us releasing our sexual frustration together. Whenever I was at work, sometimes my thoughts would drift to him and his enormous package. And I wished I worked from home just so I could stop by for some action.

He made me come quickly, his pelvic bone rubbing right against my clit as he buried me inside the door.

I came with a scream, digging my nails into his back while shuddering at the same time. My ankles locked around his waist, and I buried my face into his neck as I finished the euphoria he just gave me.

Ryker followed me immediately afterward, coming deep inside me and filling me with all of his come. He moaned against the door, his grunts just as sexy as his appearance. He kept me pinned there as he recovered, his heart racing against mine as he caught his breath.

Ryker was a god. "Jesus Christ, that was good."

"You can call me Ryker."

I rolled my eyes and released a chuckle. "Oh, shut up."

A knock sounded on the door, full of reluctance. It was a quiet tap, like the person knew we were right against the door.

Shit.

Ryker quickly set me down and pulled on his clothes.

It must be the pizza guy, so I darted into the bathroom with my clothes and quickly dressed while Ryker faced the delivery person.

"Uh...large combination?" the guy asked hesitantly.

"Yeah." Ryker's deep voice sounded confident, like he had nothing to be ashamed of.

"Let me get the change for you..."

"Keep it." Ryker shut the door.

I walked out of the bathroom with just my t-shirt on, my cheeks red with humiliation. There was no way the guy didn't figure out what we were just doing a moment ago.

Ryker popped open the lid with a proud smile on his face. "What?"

"He totally heard us."

"So what?"

"It's a little embarrassing, don't you think?"

"Not for me." He grabbed a slice and dropped it onto a plate. "I gave him a nice tip, so he'll be fine." He set the plate down in front of me before he grabbed his own slice.

I sat down on one of the barstools and devoured my piece, starving after the fucking we just did.

Ryker continued to stand, eating his pizza and making it look sexy as hell. He could be in a commercial for any pizza chain and double their sales. "How was your day?"

Nathan popped into my head, but I didn't want to talk about him. It just bummed me out. When I was with Ryker, I was happy, so I didn't want to change that. "Pretty boring. When I left work, I was going to go to the gym, but I decided to drink a bottle of wine instead."

"I think you made the right choice, for what it's worth."

"Really? Mr. I'm-in-perfect-shape?"

"Yes, I work my ass off to look like this. I'm not embarrassed about it." He grabbed another slice. "But you, on the other hand, look damn sexy without doing a thing, so just keep doing what you're doing."

"It'll catch up."

"Nah. Even if you gained a few pounds, you'd still be hot as fuck."

"You're just saying that."

"I'm really not." He took a bite before he dropped the slice onto his plate. "You're a natural beauty, you know?"

"A natural beauty?" I asked, a smile creeping into my face.

"Yeah."

"What's a natural beauty?"

He chewed for a second before he answered. "So, there are hot chicks with their perfect bodies, done hair, long legs, etc. They're your supermodels and porn stars. That's not you."

"Ouch," I said with a chuckle.

"You're a natural beauty, meaning you don't need makeup, designer clothing, any enhancement. You walk into a room, and you steal focus. People respect you. People adore you. You've got this natural grace that just makes you...special. You're the kind of woman a man wants for his wife, to be the mother of his children. You aren't the kind of woman a guy wants for the night so he can brag to his friends. You're a keeper. No man wants a one-night stand with you because they can't get enough. That's what I mean." He took another bite of his slice like he hadn't just said the sweetest thing I'd ever heard.

I stared at him blankly, feeling the blush burn in my cheeks. No one had ever said anything so sweet to me, that I was unforgettable and special. I didn't do anything to deserve such a compliment, and he blurted it out like it wasn't hard for him to say. "I...I don't know what to say to that."

"You don't need to say anything. You asked me a question, and I answered it." He kept eating like everything was normal, like he hadn't just said something that every woman wanted to hear from her significant other. "Want another piece?"

I lost my appetite after everything he'd just said. "No thanks."

***

Ryker was cuddled into my side, spooning me from behind. After another round of amazing sex, we lay together in comfortable silence. The TV wasn't on, and we just enjoyed each other's company.

"I'm gonna get some water." He kissed my hairline as he got out of bed. "Want anything, sweetheart?"

"No, I'm okay." He pulled on his sweats then left the bedroom.

The second he was gone, I missed him. The sheets were cold, and his smell didn't envelop me.

His phone vibrated on the nightstand when a message popped up. My eyes automatically went to it in reaction, and instantly, I saw the name on the screen.

Rae.

I quickly looked away and didn't read the message, out of respect for his privacy. But I still felt the pain hit me right in the gut. Jealousy washed through me like it never had before. I shouldn't care, but I couldn't help it. I did care—a lot. This was the woman he was still in love with, the only woman he'd ever loved. They obviously still kept in contact. It made me wonder how many nights he went to sleep thinking about her, wishing she were beside him instead of me.

I'd never felt so low.

I couldn't remember the last time I felt this terrible.

Must have been the night I walked in on Nathan and Lily.

I quickly got out of bed and pulled on my jeans and t-shirt, wanting to get out of there so I wouldn't have to see another text message pop up. Ryker didn't do anything wrong. I'd just gone to coffee with Nathan earlier that day. Ryker didn't owe me anything, and I knew that.

But I still wanted to leave.

I walked into the kitchen and saw him standing at the sink drinking a glass of water.

He turned to me when he realized I walked into the room. "Change your mind…why are you dressed?"

"I just remembered I need to do laundry. I'm out of everything." I did my best to lie and make it sound convincing. I slept at his place on a normal basis now, so it was unusual for me to storm out like this. "No panties, no nothing."

"Then don't wear panties." He waggled his eyebrows.

I would normally chuckle or crack a smile, but now I just wanted to go. "I'll see you later."

That reaction tipped him off. "Everything alright, sweetheart?" He walked to me where I stood in the entryway, looking me up and down with his piercing gaze.

"Yeah, I'm great. I just need to do a load. If I don't start now, it'll take forever." I rose on my tiptoes and gave him a quick kiss on the lips, trying not to picture what Rae might look like. "I'll see you later."

He snatched me by the wrist before I could walk out the open door. He yanked me back into his chest, getting a good look at my expression. "Why do I get the feeling you're lying to me?"

I wouldn't last much longer under that hot stare. "Because you just don't want me to go." I moved back into him and kissed him again, this time harder and with more passion. I had to make him think everything was okay. That was everything was perfect. Otherwise, he would drag it out of me, and it would ruin everything. He said he would never have feelings for me. If I made it awkward, he might stop our relationship altogether. I pulled away and kept my face close to his. "I won't wear panties tomorrow…and I'll be thinking of you."

***

"What's wrong?" Madeline sat across from me at our usual picnic table outside of The Muffin Girl.

"What makes you think anything is wrong?"

"I could tell just through text. You're off. Plus, the look on your face is a pretty big deal-breaker too."

Maybe I wasn't so good at appearances after all.

"Did something happen with Nathan?"

I told her everything that happened with Nathan, from our dinner together and to the present moment. "But he's not the one I'm upset about."

"Wait…why did you get coffee with him yesterday?"

"I have no idea, Maddie. He just asked me, and I couldn't say no. And I feel all these feelings that I used to feel for him… Am I the most pathetic person in the world?"

Instead of giving me shit, she sighed. "No, not at all."

"After what he did to me, I shouldn't want anything to do with him. But I'm still attracted to him. When I'm with him…it feels right. I feel like I've got my Nathan back. But I can't let that happen, right?"

Madeline took a long time to respond, probably understanding just how heavy this conversation was. "You still love him."

"I guess…" The truth was looking me right in the face. Even if I closed my eyes, the truth was still there.

"I remember how you felt about him, Austen. You were head over heels. I honestly thought you guys were meant to be. You were the ideal couple. I really thought he loved you. So I understand why you're struggling with this. I don't think it makes you stupid or weak. You really love him…even now."

"But I shouldn't, right?"

She shrugged. "I don't think love is logical. You can't control the way you feel about someone."

"So you think I should give him another chance?"

She held up her hand. "I definitely did not say that."

"So you don't think I should give him another chance?"

"Personally, no. But this is you—not me." She gave me a look full of pity, like she wished she could do more for me.

"I don't know what's wrong with me, Maddie. I don't want to feel this way."

"I know..."

"And then on top of that, I was at Ryker's last night. Everything was fine until I saw Rae send him a text message at nine in the evening."

"Who's Rae?" she asked.

"The woman Ryker is still in love with." Saying the words out loud hurt as much as they did when I said them in my head. "Ryker and I agreed to a casual arrangement, but when I saw that message, I felt terrible. I got dressed and took off."

Madeline straightened once I told her the story. "So, you have real feelings for Ryker?"

Why was my life so upside down right now? "I don't know...I thought I didn't."

"If you were that jealous over a text message, I think that's pretty obvious. What did it say?"

"I didn't look. I just left."

"So...you're into two different guys?"

I dragged my hands down my face. "I'm such a slut, I know."

"I never called you a slut," she said calmly. "But are you into two different guys? Has this thing with Ryker started to mean something to you?"

"I...I don't know." We started off as a fling, but now I spent almost every single day with him. When I didn't talk to him, I missed him. Whenever I was down, he was the first person I turned to. He'd become my closest friend in the world and the best sex I've ever had.

"Does he know how you feel about Nathan?"

I nodded. "I told him I still have feelings that I can't get rid of."

"And he told you how he felt about this Rae person?"

I nodded again.

"It sounds like you guys are in exactly the same boat."

"I suppose." I took a large bite of my muffin, needing some serious comfort food.

"Maybe your feelings for Ryker are stronger than you think they are. Think about it, you've been seeing him for months now."

"But we agreed it would never mean anything—"

"Things change, Austen. I've seen the way Ryker looks at you. You definitely aren't just a fling to him."

I remembered what Ryker said to me yesterday, that he thought of me as natural beauty. "I know he really cares about me, and we have a connection. But I don't think he wants more than what we have."

"How do you know unless you talk to him?" she countered.

I didn't know, but I suspected the answer. He still had feelings for Rae, and I still had feelings for Nathan. But whatever the two of us had together was pretty great. I wasn't sure if it would ever go anywhere, not after we agreed to be meaningless in the first place. "I don't know..."

"I would think about it. It's obvious Ryker makes you happy. I can see it written all over your face. If you're willing to give someone else a chance, I think it should be him."

"Yeah?"

She nodded. "I do. Nathan had his chance, but he blew it. I know you still love him, but he can't erase what he did. Things like that are hard to get over—no matter how much time has passed."

Chapter Nineteen

Ryker

Rae sent me a picture of Safari and Razor in ridiculous dog sweaters.

I would have smiled if Austen hadn't left so abruptly. She claimed nothing was wrong, and since she wouldn't lie to me, I believed her. But I was bummed she wouldn't be sleeping beside me tonight.

I actually liked it.

I texted Rae back after my mood got better. *Lookin' good.*

The three dots appeared before she wrote back. *Safari hates it. He ripped it off as soon as I took the picture.*

I respect him for it.

LOL. Can I call you?

I didn't want to talk to her. Every time I did, it made me miss her. But I also enjoyed our conversations, so I wanted to keep having them. I was at war with myself. *Sure.* I wondered if Zeke was fine with that. He was obviously home at this time of night.

She called me a moment later. "Yo, how's it going?"

"You can't pull off yo," I said with a laugh.

"Neither can you," she jabbed.

"Then let's agree that we both shouldn't say yo again." I lay in bed and stared at the ceiling. The sheets were bunched around my waist, but they were cold. My sleeping partner wasn't there to keep me company through the night. My king-size bed never felt as big as it did now.

"Agreed," she said with a chuckle. "What's up with you?"

"Nothing." My life was boring and uneventful. The only good thing I had was Austen—my ray of sunshine. "What's up with you?"

"Jessie finished her first trimester. Now she's starting to show."

"Good for her."

"I'm excited to be an aunt. I've already bought so many baby clothes, and I don't even know if it's a girl or a boy."

"What do you think it is?" I pictured Rae's beautiful face, the way her eyes lit up when she talked about the people she loved.

"A boy. Her belly hangs so low."

"Isn't that a myth?"

"I don't know. But I still think it's a boy either way."

I pictured Rae pregnant with Zeke's child. The other idea depressed me, so I quickly thought of something else. Our conversations were always tense no matter how much time had passed. I hadn't seen her in four months, but it didn't seem that long.

"How's it going with that lady friend of yours?"

"Austen?" I asked, vaguely remembering that I'd mentioned her.

"Yeah. You said you guys were spending time together."

"Yeah, we agreed to be fuck buddies. But we do spend a lot of time together." In fact, we spent every day together. She usually came over for dinner and sex. We had another round in the morning then she showered and headed off to work. Sometimes we went out to dinner or to a bar to watch a game. "We went car racing last weekend, and she kicked my ass." I chuckled at the memory.

"Good for her," Rae said. "I like a woman who knows how to push the pedal to the metal."

"Yeah, she's great." I wished she were there with me now.

"How long have you been seeing her?"

"About three months."

Rae paused over the phone. "Three months?"

"Yeah..."

"That's a long time to have a fling."

"She's awesome in the sack." Since it was the truth, I didn't care about saying it. "And she's really awesome. She's funny, smart, makes me feel good. She's probably my closest friend, honestly." I'd spent all evening with her, and I still missed her.

"Ryker, that sounds like more than a fling."

"It's not." I couldn't count the number of times Austen reminded me that nothing could ever happen between us. She committed to being as distant as possible. It was unlikely she would change her mind, especially since she still had feelings for her ex.

"Why are you so sure?"

I was talking about my sex life with my ex, but it didn't feel awkward anymore. "She still has feelings for her ex."

"Oh...when did they break up?"

"About three years ago."

"What?" she blurted over the phone. "And she's not over him?"

"They were engaged, but he left her for her best friend... She never got over it. I think that's why she just sleeps around, never seeing the same guy twice."

"But she's seen you more than twice."

I knew she'd made an exception for me. Actually, she'd made many exceptions for me. "She says I'm the best sex she's ever had."

"I think there's more to it than that."

"What are you trying to say, Rae?" She didn't know Austen, and she honestly didn't know much about my life anymore.

"No woman has a fling with a guy for three months without feeling something. I can guarantee she's head over heels for you, Ryker."

I chuckled because she was wrong. "Not the case with Austen."

"I know I'm right, Ryker. No way in hell is this woman immune to your charms. She's not a robot."

If she did feel something more, she hid it well.

"Ryker, how do you feel about her?"

It was starting to feel like an interrogation. "I don't know… I think she's cool."

Rae went silent over the phone again. "If you feel something for her, you should tell her. I guarantee she'll say she feels the same way."

"You don't know her, Rae. No offense."

"But I know you," she said coldly. "And you don't see the same woman for that long unless she means something to you."

She cornered me, and we both knew it. "She said she didn't want anything more, Rae. I agreed. I can't go back on my word now. Besides, I don't have anything to offer her. All I can offer her is good sex and my time. I don't love her, and frankly, she knows I still have feelings for you."

Rae was silent over the phone, obviously having no response to that.

"Honestly, I would like to give our relationship a try. I don't want her to see anyone else. I don't want to see anyone else either. But it's just too complicated. We both have feelings for other people. Neither one of us is in the right place for something serious."

"You guys are in the same situation, which I find ironic. I don't see why you can't tell her how you feel and start from there. It doesn't have to be serious. But it can be more than a fling, at least."

"What does it matter? Why don't we just keep doing what we're doing?"

"Because you don't want her to go out with some other guy, right?"

Her words hit me right in the chest. I took too long to tell Rae how I felt, and she ended up with someone else. She was reminding me of my mistake and doing her best to say it as gently as possible.

"Tell her how you feel, Ryker. Be completely honest with her. Trust me, she'll be glad to hear it."

When I thought about our time together, I knew Austen meant something to me. The relationship reminded me of what I had with Rae in some ways, but it was also better in a lot of aspects. Austen was my closest friend, the person I told everything to. I'd never had a woman in my life I was that close with—not even Rae. When Austen left in the morning, I couldn't wait until I saw her again later that night. I didn't check out other women because I didn't even notice them. Austen was the only woman I wanted to be with—I knew that much. I couldn't give her love right now because my heart was still attached to Rae. But I could give her everything else I had. "I need to think about it."

"Okay," she whispered. "I'm glad you're considering it. That tells me she really is important to you."

"Yeah..."

"Let me know what you decide."

"Okay." I missed Austen the moment she left my apartment, but I also missed the woman on the other line. How could I feel the same thing for two different people at the same time? I'd never cared enough about a single person in my lifetime, but now I cared about two different women.

How did I get here?

Chapter Twenty

Austen

I just got home from work, my unused gym bag over my shoulder, when someone knocked on my door.

Ryker wouldn't just stop by unannounced. It wasn't his style. It could be Maddie or Jenn, but they would probably give me a heads-up. If I were lucky, it would be a Girl Scout able to make me feel even worse for skipping the gym.

I checked through the peephole because, after all, this was New York City. Lots of weirdos around. I hadn't seen any in my building, but you didn't have to be a genius to sneak inside.

It was Nathan.

I wasn't sure how he knew where I lived, but it didn't surprise me that he figured it out. A phone call would have been appreciated, though. I opened the door and came face-to-face with him. "Don't show up on my doorstep ever again. If you wanna talk, call me." I came across as a little rude, but I didn't appreciate the breach of privacy.

Nathan immediately wore a guilty look. "Sorry. My friend Sam lives on your floor. I left his apartment when I saw you walk by…so I thought I would stop by and say hi. I guess you didn't see me. You looked like you were on a mission to get home."

Guilt washed over me after the snappy way I just told him off. "Oh…sorry."

"It's okay. You're right, I probably should have called."

Now that we were face-to-face on my doorstep, I didn't know what to do. I could invite him inside, but that seemed too intimate for our situation.

Nathan didn't wait around for an invite. "You wanna catch the game at Hubble? It's just down the block."

It was a sports bar near my place. I'd been there a few times.

"We can split a basket of garlic fries." He waggled his eyebrows. "And the first round is on me."

Fries and beer were something I couldn't turn down. Nathan moved his hands in his pockets, looking handsome with his broad shoulders and pretty eyes. He didn't pressure me, but he easily swayed me with his looks. "Yeah, sure."

"Cool. You wanna go now?"

I was still in my work clothes because I hadn't had the chance to change. "Just let me change, and we'll go." I left the door open and walked into my apartment, silently inviting him inside.

Nathan walked in and shut the door behind him, taking a look around my living room. He eyed the picture frames on the table, a few of me and the girls along with some college friends.

"You want anything while you wait?"

"No." He sat on the couch and pulled out his phone. "I know you're quick. I remember."

I let the comment on our former relationship slide. "Be right back."

***

After watching the game together for twenty minutes, the usual awkwardness evaporated. We fell back into the way we used to be, making jokes about the plays and the coaches. We split a basket of fries and had more beers than we should.

"Ten bucks says he makes it," Nathan said.

"There's only five seconds left on the clock."

"LeBron can do anything."

We watched the last five seconds of the game, and to my surprise, LeBron made the three-pointer while being blocked by three guys. "Damn…"

"You can keep your ten bucks. Buy me another beer instead."

I was on my third beer, and we hadn't even been sitting there for two hours. "I didn't go to the gym—again. And now I've eaten a whole basket of fries and three beers. I'm out of control."

"No, you aren't. You only live once. Eat and be happy." He clinked his beer against mine.

I smiled then took a drink. "I can drink to that."

Nathan told me about his day at work and a new billboard he was working on. I told him about my new marketing strategy and the artwork that went with it. Talking about our jobs almost seemed like a conflict of interest, but we did it anyway.

When we closed out our tab, Nathan threw his card down.

I tossed my card next to his. "We split it."

Nathan didn't argue with me, probably knowing I wouldn't let it slide. If I let him pay for it, it would seem like a date. And I didn't want this to be a date. I wasn't sure what we were doing, but we were doing it anyway.

Nathan turned on his stool and looked at me, his arm resting against the counter. "I'm doing the Manhattan marathon in a few weeks."

"You are? Good for you." It was the full twenty-six miles, a feat I could never accomplish.

"I usually jog in the morning. You wanna go for a run with me around Central Park on Saturday?"

"How far of a run are we talking?" I could do a mile, but that was about it.

He shrugged. "Maybe six."

"Yikes. That's not a run."

He smiled. "You can do it. I know you can."

"No, I know I can do it." I held my finger. "I just don't want to."

He chuckled. "We can get breakfast afterward. It'll be fun."

He still made me feel butterflies after all this time. I wanted to agree to whatever he said even though he'd done something terrible to me. I immediately forgave him when I shouldn't because I would always feel the same way about him. I would always remember the first time I looked at him. Even in that moment, I knew Nathan would be a special part of my life. "Okay...you talked me into it."

"Great." He leaned toward me and eyed my lips, just the way he used to right before he kissed me.

My heart immediately pounded with adrenaline, knowing what was going to happen next if I didn't stop it. I needed to hop out of that chair and put space between us. If I didn't, our mouths would touch, and I would be lost all over again.

But I didn't move.

Because I wanted him to kiss me.

When I didn't pull away, he pressed his mouth against mine, his lips soft and warm. His kiss was innately different than Ryker's but familiar. I felt the heat in my stomach just the way I used to. Whenever Nathan touched me, my body came to life. My breathing picked up, and I felt my body respond to him in ways it shouldn't.

But then I thought about Ryker.

His kiss was nothing like this. It was searing hot and powerful. It not only made me weak in the knees, but it made me feel safe. He wasn't just my lover, but my best friend. I was confused about my feelings for the two men, but in that moment, it became clear. I never thought about Nathan when I was with Ryker. But I always thought about Ryker when I was with Nathan.

After the kiss lasted too long, I pulled away. "I'm sorry..."

He sighed like he knew what was coming. "I should have been more patient. You just look so beautiful, and we were having a great time—"

"Ryker and I were just fooling around."

He watched me closely.

"He was never my boyfriend. He was just a friends-with-benefits type of relationship. But the more time we've spent together, the more I think it's something more than that. And kissing you makes me feel like I'm doing something wrong, like I'm betraying him."

His eyes fell in disappointment.

"I think I want to be with him..." I was so confused when I spoke to Madeline the other day. Ryker said he was still in love with Rae and he didn't want to be in a relationship. But maybe his feelings had changed the way mine had. I still had feelings for Nathan, but maybe those emotions would go away in time. "He still has feelings for his ex. I still have feelings for you. But...I'm gonna see if he wants to be something more."

Nathan sighed quietly, not bothering to hide his feelings about it. "I understand, Austen. I had my chance with you, and I blew it. I have no right to be mad or disappointed. He seems like a good guy."

"He is."

He finished the rest of his beer and set it down with a loud clank. "If you talk to him and he doesn't feel the same way, would you be willing to give me a real chance?"

That was a loaded question. "I...I don't know. Honestly, I don't know how I feel about you, Nathan. I wish I could just forget about you and not give a damn. I hate the fact that I feel this way about you. It's not fair."

Despite my insult, he didn't react. He continued to watch me with an unreadable expression on his face. Looking just as handsome as always, he stared at me. Then he rose out of his chair. "Let me know what he says..." He walked past me and left the bar.

I stayed in my chair and eyed my beer, feeling the dread well up inside of my stomach. The second I kissed Nathan, I thought about Ryker. My feelings for him had been deep below the surface for a while, I could tell. But now that I had to actually talk to him, I was nervous. What if I put my heart on the line, and he didn't feel the same way?

Chapter Twenty-One

Ryker

"You wanna make it interesting?" Liam asked as he walked beside me on the sidewalk.

"How so?"

"A hundred bucks." He waggled his eyebrows at me.

"You're prepared to lose a hundred bucks? Are you sure you can afford to spare that now that you have a girlfriend? Women are expensive."

"She's not my girlfriend—yet. And I'm not gonna lose."

We walked up to the sports bar, and I opened the door. "I'm not gonna go soft on you. I'm gonna take your cash and not feel bad about it at all."

"I'm not gonna feel bad for taking money from you either, rich bitch."

I chuckled then headed toward the bar. The game was on the TV, and people were gathered around to watch. When I stepped forward, I noticed a familiar face. With deep brown hair and a tight dress, she looked exceptional as always. I'd been meaning to talk to her since my conversation with Rae, and like it was meant to be, she was right in front of me.

But then I noticed Nathan right beside her. He was close to her, his knee touching hers. He was staring so hard at her face that I could feel tension teen feet away. His eyes moved to her lips, his intention evident.

Austen wore the exact same look.

And then Nathan leaned in and kissed her. He cupped her cheek as he deepened the passion, as he felt her soft lips with his own. I knew exactly what he was feeling because I'd kissed her so many times.

She kissed him back, her mouth moving with his like she needed him as much as he needed her.

I felt sick.

I wasn't the jealous type, so jealousy isn't what I felt. I just felt like shit.

Liam stopped next to me, watching the scene play out in front of him. "Uh..."

I couldn't stop watching them, watching the way Austen was still in love with her ex. He cheated on her with her best friend, but here she was, making out with him.

She didn't owe me anything, so I shouldn't care. She wasn't betraying me because we agreed we were just hooking up. She warned me not to fall for her. Liam did too. And now I felt light-headed and crippled.

Liam eyed me with hesitance, unsure what was going on and what I would do.

As much as I wanted to grab Nathan and yank him off of her, I didn't have the right. She wasn't my girl. So I turned around and walked out, trying to scrape the image from the inside of my brain.

I walked outside and inhaled the humid air, still feeling ice-cold. I walked past the windows, heading in the direction of my apartment with a beating heart and a raging migraine.

"You okay, man?" Liam kept up with me, still eyeing me uncertainly.

"I'm fine," I snapped, feeling anything less than fine.

Liam walked with me, silent for a while. "I don't want to be the guy who says I told you so…but I told you so. Austen is a heartbreaker. That's just how she is."

"She's not a heartbreaker. She never misled me about her feelings."

"But you fell for her anyway… I've seen it before."

I didn't fall for her. But witnessing my own reaction, I understood she meant more to me than I realized. "Liam, I'm okay. I'm just…surprised. I didn't expect her to get back together with him."

"I know...I'll have to give her a piece of my mind about it."

Now I just wanted to be alone, to go back to feeling absolutely nothing. When I left Seattle, I was completely numb. Austen was the first person to make me feel something, to make me feel something good. Now that was taken away from me. "I'll talk to you later, man." He started to walk away.

"Are you sure?" Liam asked.

"Yeah." I kept walking until I couldn't feel Liam's presence any longer. I kept replaying the image of Austen kissing Nathan in my head, torturing myself until I understood it was real—not a nightmare.

Over the course of the last three months, Austen had become my best friend. She was amazing in the bedroom, and I actually enjoyed spending time with her when we weren't screwing. It reminded me of my relationship with Rae—but better. But Austen was still in love with her ex, and now she was going to give him another try.

So she'd never felt anything for me. When she warned me that she wouldn't change her mind, I should have believed her. I shouldn't have allowed myself to develop any fondness for her.

But I failed.

I picked a random bar and walked inside, needing booze and a beautiful woman to make me feel less alone. The only woman I wanted in my bed was out kissing some other guy. Once they left the bar, they would probably hook up. They'd probably been sleeping together for a while—she just didn't tell me.

I walked up to a pretty brunette I found sitting alone. She wore a black dress with her hair pulled back in a slick ponytail. Right now, I didn't care how beautiful or unbeautiful a woman was. I just wanted someone—anyone. "Hey, beautiful. Can I buy you a drink?"

She smiled once she looked at me, obviously liking what she saw. "How about I buy you a drink instead?"

Chapter Twenty-Two

Austen

That kiss with Nathan made my body feel warm. My lips tingled from the sensation, and my breathing went haywire. I definitely felt something, just like I did when we were together.

But I felt something more for Ryker.

I was nervous to tell him how I felt. I wasn't even sure where to begin. There was a good possibility he would say he saw me as nothing more than a friend he enjoyed screwing. That sounded like something he would say. But then I thought about all the times he held me against his chest in bed, the way he kissed me when we were out to dinner, and the way he kissed my temple at the most unexpected times.

Maybe he did feel the same way.

I wouldn't know until I spoke to him.

After work, I finally summoned the courage to text him. *Hey, Sexy.*

He texted back immediately. *Hey, Stone Cold.*

Can I come by?

No gym today? I could hear his tease through the text.

You already know the answer. I smiled as I slipped my phone into my back pocket, excited to see him. Hopefully, he would just be in his sweatpants and without a shirt. That was my favorite way to look at him.

I arrived at his door a few moments later, and he let me inside. He gave me a smile and a quick hug, but he didn't kiss me.

That was odd.

"How was work?" He was in the middle of cooking. Raw chicken sat on the cutting board along with a bowl of freshly prepared marinade. The vegetables were washed and drying on a paper towel.

"Good. Pretty much the same as always." I eyed the food and felt my hunger grow. "So, what's for dinner?"

"Honey garlic chicken with rice and vegetables." He grabbed a large knife and began to slice the chicken into quarters. "I'm having a date over, and I felt like eating in tonight." He watched his hands as he worked systematically, dropping the sliced chicken into the bowl with the marinade.

I stood on the opposite side of the counter, but I suddenly felt weak. I heard what he said, but I couldn't digest it. Every syllable was too difficult to take in, too painful. "A date...?" I didn't realize he was seeing anyone else. The surprise caught me off guard, and I gripped the edge of the counter.

"Yeah. I met her last night. Her name is Cheyenne."

"Oh..." I couldn't think of anything better to say. I was more devastated than I ever could have predicted. I came over here to see if he wanted to take our relationship to the next level, but he'd spent the night with some woman. "Oh..."

He kept his eyes on his hands, like everything was perfectly normal. "So, you're back together with Nathan?" There wasn't any aggression in his tone, just pure acceptance.

"Why do you ask that?" It was random and out of the blue. I hadn't even told him I was spending time with Nathan.

"Because I saw you two kissing last night." He finally looked up from the cutting board and met my gaze. Again, there wasn't any hostility. He looked at me just as a friend—nothing more.

"You did...?"

"I went to watch the game at the bar, and when I walked in, I saw you guys going at it."

"We weren't going at it," I argued.

"Whatever," he said. "A kiss is a kiss, right?" He dropped more chicken into the bowl. "If that's what you want, that's fine with me. Just be careful. Give the relationship some time before you trust him again. That's my best advice."

"I'm not getting back together with him. It just happened..."

"But you've been spending time with him, right?"

"Well...yeah."

He finished the rest of the chicken and tossed it into the bowl where it was coated with the glaze. "I'm not angry, but I would have appreciated the heads-up. Have you slept with him?"

"No." I was offended by the question. We agreed to tell each other in the event that happened.

"Well, I slept with someone last night. So I guess we're back to condoms." He grabbed a plastic bag and transferred the chicken inside before he pushed out the air and zipped it shut. He talked like everything was fine, like this conversation was borderline boring. "That is, if you still want to keep doing this. If you're trying to make it work with Nathan, it might not be the best idea."

Now that I knew he was sleeping with someone else, I wasn't sure if I could share him. I was used to having him all to myself, to waking up with him the following morning. I saw him almost every day, told him everything about my life. But now he would do the same thing with someone else.

I shouldn't be upset because these were the terms I initiated. But the devastation crept into my veins like a poison. I would hurl at least once before the night was over.

"Austen?"

I looked up, coming back to the conversation. "Hmm?"

"Should we call our arrangement off?" He must not have a clue that I was heartbroken because he continued to talk like we were having a business meeting. There were no feelings and no emotions. Nothing at all.

"Yeah...I guess." I didn't want to think about him kissing some other woman. I didn't want to think about some other woman sleeping in the bed I slept in almost every night. Since I didn't want to share him, maybe being in this situation wasn't the best. At some point, Ryker began to mean a lot more to me than I anticipated. And if he didn't feel anything for me, it was dangerous for me to stay.

It was just like Nathan all over again.

Ryker walked away.

But I didn't have any right to be mad.

Ryker nodded then carried the cutting board to the sink where he washed it. "That's probably for the best. But we'll still each other all the time, I'm sure."

"Yeah..."

He scrubbed the board then washed his hands before he dried everything. Then he brought the vegetables and began to work on those.

The only reason why I was still there was because my legs couldn't move. I didn't know how to carry myself out of that apartment. I didn't know where to go if I didn't stay here. Ryker had become a large component of my life. But now that connection ended like the snap of a finger.

Ryker diced the vegetables like it was a normal afternoon. The knife continued to slice through the vegetables, making an audible crunching sound that was loud in my ears. I recognized the same sound from inside my chest—the sound of my breaking heart.

Ryker's story concludes in Book 7, Ray of Life.

Dear Reader,

Thank you for reading Ray of New. I hope you enjoyed reading it as much as I enjoyed writing it. If you could leave a short review, it would help me so much! Those reviews are the best kind of support you can give an author. Thank you!

Wishing you love,

E. L. Todd

Want To Stalk Me?

Subscribe to my newsletter for updates on new releases, giveaways, and for my comical monthly newsletter. You'll get all the dirt you need to know. Sign up today.

www.eltoddbooks.com

Facebook:

https://www.facebook.com/ELTodd42

Twitter:

@E_L_Todd

Now you have no reason not to stalk me. You better get on that.

EL's Elites

I know I'm lucky enough to have super fans, you know, the kind that would dive off a cliff for you. They have my back through and through. They love my books, and they love spreading the word. Their biggest goal is to see me on the New York Times bestsellers list, and they'll stop at nothing to make it happen. While it's a lot of work, it's also a lot of fun. What better way to make friendships than to connect with people who love the same thing you do?

Are you one of these super fans?

If so, send a request to join the Facebook group. It's closed, so you'll have a hard time finding it without the link. Here it is:

https://www.facebook.com/groups/1192326920784373

Hope to see you there, ELITE!

Made in the USA
Middletown, DE
18 June 2017